MAN OF HONOUR

Book Three – Final Chapter of the

Tony Simons Series

Larry & Shirley Crandell

Publishers: McNally Robinson/Larry&Shirley Crandell 2020

ISBN: 1-772803146

Edited by: Kathryn Crandell and Garry & Brenda Boese

Cover Image by Getmilitaryphotos/Shutterstock.com

"Every man's life ends the same way. It is only the details of how he lived and how he died that distinguish one man from another."

- Ernest Hemingway

Acknowledgement

I'd like to take this opportunity to thank our daughter, Katie for providing the spark that led me to write.

It started when she asked to interview me for a University paper she was writing. After hours of questions and stories, she looked at me and said "Dad you so should write a book!"

I'd also like to thank Shirley who ignited the spark when one sunny morning in May 2018, while I was sitting with a cup of coffee, she joined me with her own cup. It was an easy habit that we fell into once we had retired but this particular morning she brought a notebook with her.

She asked me not to talk to her and she fiercely started writing. About an hour later she looked up and handed me the notebook, saying "what do you think this is?"

I read the rough story and when I was done, I looked at her and couldn't help smiling. "It's me!"

She of course, knew about a lot of my past, but certainly not all and she had quite nicely turned it into fiction.

"Tony Simons was spitting mad!..." (Excerpt from "Branded," Chapter 6) And so it began. We became partners in this journey and I couldn't be happier. I believe I have truly found my "next chapter."

PROLOGUE

Tony couldn't believe the amount of snow coming down. He knew this was going to take a bit. He looked around and noticed a large transport truck moving towards him on the opposite side of the road some 100 yards away.

He turned back to look at his car and that's all he remembered!...

Lieutenant Evans looked closely at him and told him to relax; it was a lot to take in. She reminded him that he was a member of the military and the military takes care of their own...

All passengers and crew are to report to their lifeboat stations and prepare to abandon ship! "Was he hearing this correctly?"...

The ferry's massive horns started to call out into the darkness and suddenly flares were being ignited and rocketed into the night sky to explode into massive stars several hundred feet in the air. This wasn't a drill. This ship was really going down! "What the hell happened?"...

As Tony weaved his way through the throngs of women, beggars and merchants, an old bent over Bedouin man bumped into him and stood his ground. Before Tony could say he was sorry, the hooded man, who was not really looking at him said in a low voice "$800 USD for your mask soldier man, $1000 USD for any others that you have. We know who you are"...

Chapter 1

It was a beautiful day for flying, with bright sunny skies and huge white puffy clouds rolling by in the distance. The giant shiny bird screamed down the runway grabbing at the air trying to climb into the sky and escape the ground. The power of the mighty engines pushed the monster forward and the people inside were forced back into their seats. The nose of the huge aircraft was the first to leave the ground while speed and power pushed the rest of the bird up into the sky, finally made a gentle turn to the left and continued to climb and head into the sun westbound.

The flight was to take five hours, and during that time Tony introduced himself to his seat partner, an elderly lady named Rose Thompson. Rose was from Toronto and she was heading to Vancouver to visit her grandkids and see the Pacific Ocean. Tony said that he had not seen the ocean either but would someday. She smiled and told him he looked very handsome in his uniform and wished him well in his new career. Tony thanked her for her kindness and turned away to spend most of the flight quietly looking out the window and thinking about what brought him to this place and time; Port Nichols, Mark, Lucifer's Army and the nightmares that happened there were still fresh in his mind. Things could have been very different for him if he had made the wrong choices.

He watched the land below change from concrete cities to great lakes, dense wooded areas and then miles upon miles of flat farmland. Things changed again, this time mountain ranges started to form with what seemed to be hundreds of miles of rivers weaving through them. Tony knew he was getting close, when in the midst of the mountains below he could see a semi desert area and the plane started descending between two mountains and before he knew it Tony landed at Fulton Field Airport, just outside Kamloops, B.C.

He said goodbye to Mrs. Thompson and wished her well. After finding his bags he began to look for a cab, when he spotted an older man in a Corporal's work dress waving him over. Tony guessed the friendly old Corporal to be fifty something; around 5'4 with grey curly hair on his head and chest. He had leathery tanned skin and one or two faded tats on his right arm that Tony couldn't make out but were probably older than he was. His work boots looked like they hadn't seen polish for years and his uniform had seen better days.

He smiled as Tony came closer and Tony could tell right away that they were going to be great friends.

"Hey there Private, I was beginning to wonder where you had got off to. Welcome to Kamloops, Simons. My name is Bill Taylor. You can call me Billy. They sent me here to pick you up and get you back to the Station. We thought you might get lost."

CFS (Canadian Forces Station) Kamloops was located 14 miles from the City, most of that up a series of mountain roads that produced quite a view. Billy knew the area like the back of his leathery hands. He drove the military van through town, across a wooden red bridge and out into the mountains and desert area to start the climb up to the Radar Site. The road wound around smaller mountains and gullies to enter into a large flat valley where cowboys grazed their cows. They had been climbing for a while so Tony was surprised to see this large flat area.

Looking out the front window, Tony could see the Radar Site off in the distance. It sat on the top of a tall mountain that Billy said was called "Lolo." He told Tony that its elevation was 5735 feet and the Radar Site had been built in 1957. It was spectacular and reminded Tony of Lac

St Denis. There were three white golf balls sitting on top of a mountain. The difference here was that this was "his" Site, his home.

Billy saw him looking at the Site with amazement. "Pretty, isn't it, Tony?" he said. Tony just nodded and continued to stare.

More turning, winding and climbing brought them finally to the Station and the main gate where Tony met Percy, an old Ukrainian Commissionaire who had been an officer in an Army in another land long ago.

It was Friday evening and Tony wasn't to report in to the Headquarters building and the DMCC (Data Maintenance Control Centre) at the top of the mountain until Monday morning.

Tony stood at the main gate and looked onto Kamloops Station. It was pretty much what he had expected, small and a little dated. There were three barrack blocks, married quarter trailers, a Mess Hall, a Supply Stores' building, a motor compound and the Headquarters Building, along with three ranks clubs for drinking. The Station was surrounded by forests on three sides and in the back, there was a road leading into the woods and up to the Radar Site that was still three miles away and several thousand feet up.

He was given a room in the barracks by the Duty Corporal and was told to relax and go to the Mess for a beer. He stood in the doorway and looked into what was his first very own room. It was around 10 by 10 with a single bed and chair in the corner. Plain, old brown curtains hung from a steel rod on a window that looked out, not to the beautiful mountains and trees that surrounded the Station, but to the next building's wall, some 20 feet away. In Tony's eyes, it was better than a room at the Holiday Inn. This was his room.

That weekend Tony met most of the people that were posted there and a few who were not. The Mess was a popular place to be on the weekend.

He met the guys that were living in the barracks and most of the men he'd be working with at the top of the hill. They greeted him warmly and advised him right away that the new guys buy the first rounds and maybe a few more. Tony quickly came to the realization that there were a lot of hard-core drinkers here and the Mess was always busy.

The weekend was a blur, but Tony held his own and survived. He reported in on Monday morning and met the Station Commander, a Major named Brayden. He was a retired Navigator who got posted to the Station for some unknown reason. Rumour had it that he had gotten drunk at some party in Ottawa and got a little handsy with the Squadron Commander's wife.

Brayden hated the Station but loved the game of golf and managed to play three times a week to avoid doing any work. He had memberships with all the courses within 100 miles of the Station. He shut the Station down many times to play in tournaments around the area.

Anyone that played or was interested in the game became Brayden's posse and played every tournament. If you didn't play, you ended up working extra shifts for the guys who did play. Tony would wise up to this quickly,

Chapter 2

Tony's first ride up the back road to the Radar Site was on Monday morning. Anyone working the dayshift rode up the hill in a big military bus with about 20 or so military personnel and civilians.

Tony was not prepared for the next 45 minutes from hell. It was a dirt road, steep and narrow and the bus laboured to negotiate the many corners and switchbacks. Occasionally, the bus popped out of the trees and looked like it was going to drive right over the cliff because there were no guard rails. If you were lucky enough to get a window seat, you would be able to look down a hundred feet or more in some spots and pray the driver was skilled at what he did. At times the road was very rough because the rain the night before had washed some of it away and exposed sharp rocks underneath that had been thrown from the tires and smashed into the undercarriage. It was a harrowing ride for Tony and he was never happier to finally round a bend and see the Radar Site in front of him for the first time.

When Tony had boarded the bus at the Station, he hadn't noticed the driver, but as he left the bus he did. It was Billy and he winked at the young serviceman as he went by.

Tony was met at security by his first new Crew Chief, Master Corporal Cecil Biggs, "Cece" to his friends he said. He was in his late 40's with thinning black hair and a massive black mustache. He was taller than Tony, thin and wiry. Cecil had been in the military for over 25 years and he was looking at retirement soon. He introduced Tony to the rest of the crew and toured him around the operations area which was to be his home for the next four years.

The rooms were dark and the green glow of the screens cast an eerie light on everything. Guys were watching the scopes and tracking little blips on screens that seemed to move as the sweeping arm from the scope passed over it. Phones were ringing; people were talking into headsets and writing backwards on plexiglass boards.

To Tony it was glorious. He had worked hard and now he was finally here.

Tony's shift was easy with plenty of time off and the work was always interesting. The guys were great to work with and gave him many opportunities to show himself and try to advance.

He always got a thrill watching the screens when a Russian Bomber accidently entered Canadian Airspace and 22nd NORAD (North American Aerospace Defence) Command out of North Bay would scramble a fighter to intercept it and send it packing.

Tony's favourite thing to do when he wasn't busy on the scopes was to walk out on the catwalk that surrounded the tower and look out onto the mountains 100 miles in all directions. Tony liked Kamloops and settled in fast.

For the first couple of years Tony's life was work, time off and hard drinking. If he wasn't drinking in the Mess he could be found in downtown Kamloops with his friends at a bar called The Stockman's, dancing and chasing girls or getting into fights because they were chasing girls.

Kamloops was a small city located in the centre of the Province of B.C. It was western in many ways and had a lot of ranches and cowboys. It wasn't surprising to see a horse or two in town on the weekend. Everywhere you looked you could see local natives because the city and the surrounding lands were owned by at least three different tribes. People were friendly and always said hello and tipped their hats when they passed by.

Located in a semi-desert area, Kamloops enjoys mild weather most of the year, but in the summer it gets hot. Most of the city locals and Station personnel could be found swimming or tubing down the Thompson River to escape the heat. It wasn't unusual to see them diving off the red wooden bridge.

On hard-core weekends the guys would go to a lower class bar located at the end of the main drag called The Leonard where they would be entertained by the local Red Hand Motorcycle Club and the women that road with them. They tried to make money and get booze any way they could from threatening unknowns that came in for a beer and a peek to getting their old ladies up on stage to grind around and take their clothes off along with the local native girls.

Tony found out just how hard core these ladies were one night as they tried to outdo one another by trying to remove a drunken guy's glasses without using their hands. These girls were hard and they played hard. It occurred to Tony that if he wanted to stay healthy and in the military he should stay clear of these soiled doves at all costs.

Chapter 3

Tony really liked his first posting and the people that worked there with him. He tended to hang around with four guys more than the others, mainly because two of them had cars but they genuinely liked each other. He had become friends with everybody that lived on the Site and became aware of all of their personalities over time.

His friends, Don, Earl, Mike and Gordie, were just young privates that wanted to be in the military and wanted to have fun. They were genuinely interested in what the military had to offer them. Others on the Site were of various ages and ranks and personal situations, each with their own stories about what brought them to Kamloops.

Tony would sit in the Junior Ranks Mess after every shift and quietly listen to the stories from the older members complaining about their jobs, their lives or their family situations. The Mess was the centre of the universe for this small Radar Site and everything else seemed to circle around it.

If you wanted to know what was going on, you just had to sit back, watch and listen. Watching and listening were Tony's strengths. He would sip his rum and coke and look around the crowded room, trying to figure out what was behind the faces he saw there. Most of the guys were easy to read. They were just putting in time.

Danny, the cook, mostly drank alone but he liked it that way. However, an older man, a Master Corporal seemed to be pretty easy going and got along with everyone but never drank. He would order a Ginger ale and sip it most of the night while exchanging pleasantries with everyone in the bar. His name was Floyd Finn. He had curly, grey and ginger hair, around 6 foot or so, leathered face, really bright eyes and was always smiling like he knew something nobody else did.

His room was at the back of the barrack block away from the youngsters, he'd say they were too damn noisy.

Tony liked the old Master Corporal and made it his mission to get to know him.

Floyd didn't drink, but he did have a gift. He could play golf like a pro and this got the Station Commander's attention right away. Floyd and Brayden would play golf at least three times a week, not including the tournaments on the weekends. They would play all day if they could.

Brayden would get drunk after a game and Floyd would drive him home.

Tony was sure Floyd knew all of Brayden's secrets, but he wasn't talking.

One Thursday evening Tony found himself in his room, listening to the radio and thinking about Floyd. "What the hell." he thought. "He was only just down the hall. What better time to see him and strike up a conversation."

Tony walked down the long hallway and found himself in front of Floyd's door. He knew Floyd was in his room because he could hear the radio playing country music.

Tony knocked a little too loudly and Floyd came quickly to the door with a questioning look in his eye. He recognized Tony immediately and his expression turned from questioning to a warm smile. "What's up, youngster?" he said. "Are you lost?" as he turned and stretched out on his bed again.

"No Floyd," Tony answered quickly. "Just thought I'd say hi; I knew you were home."

"Come in and sit down, Tony, thanks for coming by."

Floyd was eyeing his visitor. Tony was lost for small talk, but a light came on and he asked Floyd without thinking "can you teach me how to play golf? It looks like a great game."

Tony wasn't looking at Floyd but around the room, trying to take everything in at one glance. It was a larger room than his but with fewer things in it, bed, dresser, closet, night stand and lamp. Wait! Something was out of place! Tony's eyes returned to the dresser and the single object that sat on top of it, a large single bottle of Crown Royal.

The words came out of his mouth before his mind kicked in. "You don't drink Floyd, what the hell is that?" he asked.

Floyd smiled a little to himself before he answered. "That is none of your business Mr. Simons, but since you asked, I feel like telling you. That's my 'conscience bottle.' It's there to remind me of a dark place I used to live in and what hard drinking did to me and what it cost. I'm five years sober right now and feeling pretty good about myself. We will leave it at that. Now what's this about learning to golf?"

Their friendship was cemented there and then and lasted for the entire time Tony was at the Site. He and Floyd would practice his stance and drive golf balls into the woods from the baseball diamond located at the back of the Station.

Tony practiced for hours and started to show a pretty good short game when putting on a small nine-hole course in town. Tony listened to what Floyd had to say, not only about the game of golf but about growing up in the military and making choices.

Chapter 4

Time moved on and Tony was eventually promoted to Corporal. He used this opportunity to buy his first car and was proud as hell of it. It was a 1972 AMC Gremlin X with a three speed transmission and a 304 V-8 that was built for speed. It even had denim seat covers!

The guys at the Station thought it was the ugliest car they had ever seen, but Tony loved it. The car gave Tony the opportunity to travel around more and he took full advantage of it. He drove all over B.C. from Vancouver Island to Fernie and the Crows Nest Pass. Tony loved to travel.

Tony planned a trip to Edmonton over Christmas to meet a friend of his and spend the holidays with his family. It was just supposed to be a week away and then back to start another shift, but it didn't turn out that way.

On the morning of the trip Tony woke to find fresh snow on the ground and the temperature around 35 degrees. It was going to take him eight and a half hours to drive to

Edmonton, maybe a little longer, depending on the weather and the roads. He was used to distance driving by then. All he needed to do was to stop for breaks and dinner and he'd be there.

He left the Station at 0600 hours knowing it was supposed to be a bright sunny day, and looking forward to the trip. He had decided earlier to drive through Jasper National Park on his way to Edmonton to save a little time and see the sights.

As he got closer to Jasper the weather started to change and the snow began to fall heavily. He drove through Jasper and another half hour or so then slowed down considerably, because it was really coming down and he was considering turning back to Jasper to wait out the storm.

The town was 17 miles back and if he turned now, he was sure he'd make it. It was too late. Tony could feel the car lose traction as he started to make a long sweeping left hand turn around a sloped opening in the tree line; the car slid into the ditch and came to rest on a 45 degree incline three feet down.

Tony wasn't hurt, but he knew he wasn't going to be able to drive out of the mess. There was a lot of snow down by this time, with no sign of letting up. The only vehicles that were still moving were heavy transports and they were few and far between. He knew he'd have to flag one down and get back to town. He needed a tow-truck.

Five minutes later, Tony found himself in a transport truck heading for Jasper, in search of a tow truck. The trucker told Tony that the roads were getting really bad and if he didn't act fast, he'd be spending the night in Jasper or maybe longer.

Back in town he found a tow truck and off they went to retrieve his car.

Tony had decided to return to Jasper with his car and wait out the storm in front of a warm fireplace and maybe find some company. He would phone his friend, Sean, in Edmonton and let him know he wasn't going to be there today and if the storm got any worse, he would be heading back to Kamloops.

The tow truck arrived back at Tony's car in about an hour and in that time the snow had just about completely covered the Gremlin. The driver hooked up his cable to Tony's car and was slowly trying to pull it from the ditch.

The slope was such that the driver had to position the truck fully in the driving lane, which bothered Tony because of the other trucks rolling by and the fact that the tow truck driver did not have the hazard lights flashing on the top of the truck.

It was a slow process and it was taking forever. There was no place for Tony to stand safely. He moved forward of the truck about twenty feet and watched the activity from the side of the ditch.

Tony couldn't believe the amount of snow coming down. He knew this was going to take a bit. He looked around and noticed a large transport truck moving toward him on the opposite side of the road some 100 yards away.

He turned back to look at his car and that's all he remembered!

Chapter 5

Tony woke up in the Jasper hospital three days later. His head was swimming, he was floating and he was numb. Tony opened an eye slowly and found a nurse standing over him telling him not to move.

She explained to him that he had been in an accident and had to lie perfectly still. His face was swollen and he couldn't open one of his eyes but he managed to tell the nurse to look in his wallet and find his leave pass. The world began to spin again and Tony found himself falling into darkness and then nothing.

Two more days went by before he opened his swollen eyes and remembered where he was. He had been in an accident and he was now in a hospital. As his vision cleared, he noticed two people in the room, both watching him intently.

The man leaned forward and said he was the doctor that was in the emergency room when Tony was brought in. He started to tell Tony that he had been in an accident involving a transport truck that had jack knifed and slid into the ditch hitting Tony like a baseball and knocking him 40 feet into the tree line. The snow landing had saved him, but he was badly injured and had to lie still.

The doctor went on to tell Tony that his collar bone was shattered and many of his ribs were cracked or broken. He had cuts to his face, arms and legs, but they would heal in time.

The doctor stepped back and a woman in a military uniform leaned over him. She told Tony that the hospital had contacted Base Edmonton about the accident and told them that they had a Corporal Simons here recovering and they had dispatched her to supervise his transport to the hospital at Base Edmonton.

Her name was Evans, Lieutenant Evans. She had been gathering information on the accident while Tony was unconscious. She began telling him what had happened and how lucky he was to be alive.

The transport came around a long winding bend and lost traction with the trailer he had been pulling. It slid sideways across the road and into the ditch, continuing to slide down the road hitting Tony a glancing blow to his right side, knocking him into the woods.

The transport continued on its path hitting and destroying Tony's car and the tow truck at the same time. When the truck finally stopped, the driver radioed the police and ran to the tree line to try and help Tony and then the tow truck driver.

Tony lay there in his bed and tried to remember, but it was not there. He also tried to come to the realization that he had been in a bad accident and he was truly lucky. It saddened him that the Gremlin was gone, but at least the driver of the tow truck was ok. "Now what?" he thought. "What was he going to do now?"

Lieutenant Evans was watching him and told him to relax. It was a lot to take in, in a short period of time. She reminded him that he was a member of the military and the military takes care of their own.

He closed his eyes and woke the next day in horrible pain. The nurse gave him something in his IV and everything became "nice" again.

The Lieutenant had not been idle while he slept. She was trying to arrange transport for Tony and herself to Edmonton as soon as possible. It came down to two possibilities and then to one because the weather had grounded the use of a military helicopter.

It was decided the train was the only way and they would be moving out in the morning.

A sleeper birth was booked and Tony was to be transported to the station very early. Three hours later, they'd be in Edmonton and at the military hospital. So the plan was laid out.

The next morning Tony was heavily drugged and put into a back brace for stability before leaving the hospital. He was carried on a stretcher to the ambulance and loaded onto the train with little to no problems. He was unaware that the nightmare would continue for 14 more hours.

The train left late from Jasper and got a half mile down the tracks before falling off because of the snow. Another three hours later they started off only to fail to stay on the tracks.

They say things happen in three's and Tony's adventure was ringing true. The train left the tracks a third time. By now Tony had to be medicated again, the pain was increasing with every hour.

They made it to Edmonton 11 hours late and in the heaviest snow storm the city had seen in some time.

The military ambulance that was to meet them at the station had left hours ago. Tony's transport was to be the back of a station wagon loaned to the Lieutenant by the Commissionaire at the Station.

Chapter 6

By this time, Tony was in and out of consciousness and was unaware of what was going on.

Two military police cars and an old station wagon rolled out of the train station at one in the morning in an evil snow storm, heading down the main street for a three mile ride to the Base.

Fate was not ready to let Tony get to safety yet. A mile from the Base, the station wagon blew a tire and began to spin in full circles down the main street of Edmonton coming to rest next to a huge pile of snow that the plows had placed on the corner.

Tony was only vaguely aware of what was going on as they hauled him out of the car and loaded him in a Base ambulance that finally got to them.

He was rushed to emergency and loaded onto a gurney so they could roll him into the hospital.

Tony had been without medication for at least six hours now and was heaving in pain. The doctors had been waiting all day for him to get there. When his doctor got closer, he noticed Tony was wearing a back brace. He told the nurse to "get that damn thing off him!"

He wanted to know how long Tony had been wearing it and had it ever been adjusted at any time. Lieutenant Evans said that he had had it on all the time with no adjustments at all.

The doctor moved forward and took over for the nurse cutting Tony out of the brace with a scalpel. He checked his circulation in his right arm and found it cold and badly colored. The doctor shook his head, swore to himself and moved Tony into the examination room to really look him over.

He woke the next day, in his own room with a military nurse watching his every move. He was mildly medicated and could understand the nurse when she said that he had been through a horrible ordeal, but things were going to be much better.

The doctor came in that afternoon and introduced himself as Captain Lowry and told Tony that he was going to take good care of him.

He told him to try and move around a bit and take stock. Tony knew he was badly hurt and he mentally checked himself over. He knew that some of him was broken and bruised, but for some reason he could not move his right arm. Worse yet, he couldn't feel his right arm.

Panic set in quickly and for the first time in Tony's life, he was really scared. The doctor explained that his collar bone was crushed and they could not cast or pin anything. He would have to stay on his back for an unspecified amount of time for his bones to knit, his cuts to heal and then lots of rehabilitation. As for the right arm, that was another story.

The doctor sat down and looked right at Tony before he began. "They should not have put you in that back brace Tony, let alone for that amount of time. The circulation in your right arm was cut off for many hours and damage to the nerves and muscles because of the lack of blood seems extensive."

Tony was shaking "what do you mean doc?"

"We don't know. Time will tell and we have a long way to go." The doctor told him to try and relax and he would stop in later to check on him.

Tony lay there on his back, alone in his room looking at the ceiling. It was so quiet. The room was stark and too white. He could hear the hospital and worst of all he could smell that hospital smell. It was starting to sink in. The only thing he could think was "oh my god."

Tony's friend in Edmonton, Sean, found out what had happened to him and came to visit him every chance he got and told him that he had contacted Kamloops and got a hold of Tony's boss. Cecil had told Sean to tell Tony to stay strong and get back as soon as he could and that he owed the whole crew many beers for covering all his shifts.

Chapter 7

Days led to weeks and weeks led to months but Tony wasn't going anywhere soon.

In time his collarbone healed and his breathing was better because his ribs had healed but his right arm was another story. It lay there and didn't move. The colour had come back and it was warm to touch, but that was it. There was no feeling and no movement. The doctors were always checking it with needles to see if the dead areas were reacting to pain to no avail.

The worst day of Tony's life was the morning that the doctor came to his room, checked his arm and had a terrifying conversation with him about the possibility of taking it. The doctor told Tony that he knew that it was a lot to take in and he would send someone around to talk more about it.

Alone in his room, Tony was freaking out inside. For some time now he had been able to get up and move around on his own, but every time the arm hit him in the side he was reminded of the doctor's words.

That afternoon he was sitting in his chair, looking out the window onto the Base, watching military people going on with their lives. His mind raced, "was he going to be able to continue his career?" Tony was coming to terms with the fact that it could all be over.

He was deep in thought as he looked out the window and didn't hear the knock at his door, or see a man enter and move toward him.

Tony turned and was startled to see a rare visitor. This was not just anybody. This was a priest! Tony's history with priests wasn't the greatest and he felt himself getting angry, but something inside him told him to calm down and take a breath. This was a military priest, a pastor. Tony wasn't sure whether this made a difference.

He was about 35 or 40, short with a barrel chest and big hands. His short hair was starting to grey, but his eyes were bright blue and friendly. His smile was, Tony thought, genuine.

He walked up to Tony and introduced himself as Pastor Winthrop, but Tony could call him Jerry. He had been in the building with his wife who had fallen down and injured herself and had heard the hospital had a long-term guest that might need to "talk."

Tony knew he was stringing him a tale. He was sure the doctor had contacted the Pastor and sent him to talk to him.

Jerry came over next to Tony and sat in another chair. "If I knew you were here, I would have visited a long time ago." The Pastor's tone was easy and Tony could see that this person was genuinely interested in hearing his story.

"Been here as long as they say?" Jerry asked.

Tony nodded, "eight months so far."

The Pastor was taken aback by the answer. He knew it had been awhile, but Tony's answer caught him off guard.

Jerry came closer, "what the heck happened to you?"

Tony took a deep breath, looked at the man's face across from him and it was like a damn burst inside him. The whole terrible chain of events came pouring out of him. The truck, the accident, nightmares he had been having and finally, the doctor's words that burned into his mind. "We might have to take your arm."

The Pastor could see that Tony was visibly upset but he could also see that he was breathing easier now that he had talked about the nightmares and his arm.

They talked for quite awhile before the Pastor said that he had to go and see to his wife. He said he would be back the next day for sure.

True to his word, Jerry showed up early the next day and entered Tony's room without knocking and with deliberation in his steps.

He walked right up to Tony's bed and pulled a chair up close to talk to him. "I made a few calls to some friends I know in the states. They run a big rehabilitation facility for sports jocks and after kicking your situation around a bit they came up with an idea for you to try. I'm not saying that it's a miracle cure Tony, and it's going to take a lot of work on your part, but it's a shot."

Tony couldn't believe what he was hearing. "What is it Pastor? Whatever it is, I'm in!"

The Pastor reached into his pocket and took out a yellow tennis ball. He moved forward and put the ball in Tony's right hand and told Tony to reach over with his left and grip the hand holding the ball. "Now squeeze the hand holding the ball and keep squeezing it until you can't stand it. Then squeeze some more. The arm needs exercise Tony and stimulation, a lot of it. It isn't like your calendar's full, so you should have plenty of time to do this all day, every day."

Tony looked at the ball and then at Jerry. "Okay" he said. "They're not taking my arm without a fight."

Jerry told him that he would check back with him in a day or two and asked if he could bring him anything.

"Cigarettes" Tony answered, "I'm dying for a smoke."

And so it began. Tony worked that ball for hours on end and days on end waiting for some type of sign that things were different. He would squeeze that ball as hard as he could and move his arm around in circles and up and down until his left arm ached.

Jerry would come in to see him and bring him magazines and cigarettes, all the while checking his progress.

A couple of months had gone by with no visible change and Tony was having a mental battle in his head as to whether he should continue the exercises or throw the damn ball out the window and surrender to the inevitable.

Then on one of those trying days, Tony lay back on his bed trying to be positive when his right arm slid off the side of the bed and hit the night stand. His hand went by, but his little finger hit the edge of the table and Tony felt a slight tingle!

He sat up and grabbed his right hand and examined it closely. It looked the same, but he could slightly feel the tip of his finger. Tears ran uncontrollably as he called for the nurse and broke the news to her. She gave Tony a hug and said she would contact the doctor immediately to let him know.

Word spread quickly around the hospital about Tony's breakthrough and it wasn't long before Jerry came running through the door with a big smile on his face. "You did it Tony! You did it! Keep it up, I think you've got this licked, my friend."

"I owe it all to you, Jerry, thank you!"

Sean too, had heard about the miracle and ran into Tony's room. "What the hell, man, what happened?" he yelled.

Tony explained what had happened. Sean stayed most of the day talking to his friend, and vowed to contact Kamloops and give them the good news.

Now the work really began for Tony. His workout routine and rehab schedule stepped up. He began to work his hand and arm harder than ever before.

The doctors were amazed with the breakthrough and Tony's progress was monitored every day. It was true, the feeling and the movement were returning to his arm. It was slow, but it was happening.

He was progressing at a steady rate. Each day a little more of him seemed to come alive. It was like when your foot goes to sleep and when waking it tingles. This is what was happening to Tony's arm.

Between the tennis ball and a light set of dumbbells, Tony was back and eventually ready to go back to work!

Chapter 8

The doctor contacted the Station about Tony's recovery and requested Travel Orders for his return. The doctor came to Tony's room and told him he'd be leaving in 48 hours. He would be transferred to transit barracks to await his travel day. Right now he had a phone call from his friends at the Station. They had heard he was coming back and wanted to congratulate him.

He walked to the office and picked up the receiver. A familiar voice came over the line and Tony smiled to himself, thinking he'd be home soon.

The voice on the phone was his Crew Chief, Cecil Biggs and he could hear the guys calling out to him in the background.

"We were pretty concerned for a long time, Tony," his Crew Chief said. "You gave us quite a fright. Glad to hear that you've recovered and will be back here in a day or two.

The guys want to say a few words and then we'll all see you at the airport."

The other two crewmen got on the phone then and wished him well. They told him that he had scared the shit out of them. "Get your ass back here, Simons! We've been working here short-shifted ever since you decided to slack off."

Tony laughed and thanked the guys for calling. He would be back to the Station Monday. Cecil said that he'd be at the airport but for now just take it easy and pack up.

Tony packed his meager belongings and before leaving his room he stopped and looked around at what had been his world for the previous 13 months and some days. It seemed smaller now and more sterile than he remembered, but it was time to get back to the real world and put this behind him.

He walked to the reception area and said goodbye to the doctors and nurses that had helped him all the many months. He had mixed emotions about leaving but climbed into the Base taxi and never looked back.

Transit barracks was just that, a bed in a line of beds, but Tony loved it, knowing it was only for a night or two and then off to the airport.

He was just coming back from lunch when he saw a familiar face pull up in front of the barracks, get out of a car and walk quickly toward him.

"Thought I was going to miss you Tony," Jerry said as he shook his hand and slapped his back. "That's a pretty strong grip you've got there, son."

Tony genuinely liked this man. He had been the main driver in his recovery and he knew he would not have made it if not for him.

"Just wanted to say goodbye and have a safe trip!" Jerry was still shaking his hand. "You and I have been through a time or two and I am glad I was able to help in my small way. You still have the ball, right?" Jerry asked.

Tony got his hand back and reached in his pocket to retrieve the ball. "I will never be without it, Pastor. It saved my life and so did you. I will never be able to repay you for all you have done." Tony said as he looked fondly at the Pastor.

Jerry looked quickly at his watch and said that he had to go. Tony and Jerry shook hands again and Jerry moved to his car and opened the door. Before climbing in he turned back to his friend on the sidewalk and said "there is something you can do for me Corporal Simons. Go to church some time. You didn't think I did this all on my own, did you?" With that he started the car and was gone.

Chapter 9

There was nothing left to do now but to go home, to Kamloops. It had been nearly 14 months of his life he would never get back but also he would never forget.

Surprisingly, the flight was short. The plane had barely left the ground when the stewardess ran down the aisle asking if anyone wanted water, matches or mints and then it was "fasten your seatbelts we're coming into Fulton Field, Kamloops!"

He stepped out of the plane and looked over to the fence to see more people than he expected to see. The Station had supplied a small crew bus to pick him up and it had a half a dozen guys he knew from his crew. They were all cheering, clapping and waving at him as he made his way into the baggage area.

It was weird. He felt like a rock star but he knew these people were genuinely happy to see him back. He was also happy to be back at last. Cecil Biggs and two other guys he worked with were in the terminal waiting for him with smiles, handshakes and slaps on the back.

"Good to see you guys" Tony said. "I sure am glad to be back. Let's get the hell out of here!"

Like normal, Bill Taylor was driving the bus and he gave Tony a smile and a wink as he boarded his military limousine. It was near full on the bus and Tony was mobbed as he made his way down the short aisle. He was really happy to see them all and got a little teary-eyed thinking that he truly had a family now, a military family. Tony could not have been happier as he looked around at his friends' smiling faces.

Something was out of place though, but he couldn't put his finger on it. Then like locating a missing piece of a puzzle, Tony realized who was missing. "Where's Floyd?" he asked, turning to Cecil.

Cecil's smile turned to a more serious frown as he explained to Tony that Floyd was drinking again and had moved downtown to be with his ex-wife.

The word was that she had phoned him after being away for some years and had asked him for money. She had been living in Vancouver and had not worked in some time. She was being thrown out of her flat and wanted Floyd to buy a bus ticket to Kamloops for her.

Everybody in the Station knew that Floyd was heart-broken when his wife had left him for a younger guy, some time back. Floyd thought she had left because of his drinking so he had quit soon after that.

It wasn't more than a week after the phone call that Floyd moved downtown and was hardly seen again on the Site unless he was working except for the time that he brought her up to the Site one Friday night for TGIF (Thank god it's Friday).

They had come roaring into the parking lot in an older red Fairlane Convertible and screeched to a stop in front of the Mess. Angy, his wife, was dressed up like a three dollar tramp with tight jean shorts and a yellow flowered blouse tied in the front. She wore bright red lipstick and nails to match her red hair that was tied back in a ponytail. Her sunglasses hid her bloodshot eyes, but she was all over Floyd like a back street hooker. She was biting his ear as they drove up to the mess and she could see that they were being watched from the front bay windows.

She smiled at the guys who were peering at her and climbed slowly out of the car over top of the door, giving them all plenty to look at.

They entered the bar and ordered Crown Royals straight up and found a table in the corner. Floyd wasn't drinking at that time but she was pounding them back and playing peak-a-boo with the younger privates sitting across from them making sure they all got a good look.

Floyd finally noticed the activity, got really pissed off and challenged the young men for leading his Angy on. He was asked to leave, which he did, swearing like a madman. As Angy left she turned to look back at the table of young guys and blew them a kiss.

No one had seen Floyd since that night, other than at work.

The guys could see he had changed and not for the better. He was thinner, his face was gaunt and his eyes were bloodshot all the time. He hardly spoke to anyone but worst of all, they could smell booze on his breath. He was a mess.

His close friends tried to talk to him but he was having none of it.

When Cece was finished, all Tony could say was "Jesus Christ."

Tony forgot about Floyd during the rest of the bus ride. Everyone was laughing and trying to talk to him all at the same time.

At the Site Tony reported to Commandant Brayden, who shook his hand and welcomed him back. He was leaving Brayden's office, when he was stopped at the door and told to fly next time. Tony agreed.

It took a week for Tony to get back into the routine of working on the Radar Site, but like all things you enjoy, it comes back quickly. He liked talking to the people in the Mess Hall. It was a common area where people could come together to talk about the day they just had or at breakfast to talk about what was ahead of them.

Tony liked breakfast most of all. The smell of fresh coffee and frying bacon when you opened the door was like a drug to him and he couldn't get enough of it. Today he was going to have sausages and eggs with pancakes and maple syrup.

The cooks here were first rate and Tony had gotten to know them all, but the one he enjoyed talking to most was Danny Leader. He was a civilian cook, contracted to the Site to cook for the men that lived in barracks.

He was a tall thin man, in his late 40's with receding thin brown hair, and a big long narrow nose that balanced a pair of black rimmed glasses with thick lenses.

Danny didn't talk to many people on the Site. He pretty much kept to himself and did his job. If he wasn't in the

Mess Hall cooking, you would find him in his room or rarely in the ranks' club, having a beer.

Danny's room was across the hall from Tony and they always exchanged pleasantries in the hall or common wash areas.

A week or so after he got back, Tony was in his room at the end of the day listening to his radio, when he heard a light knock on his door. He opened it to find Danny standing in front of him. A quizzical look came over his face. This was a first. Tony broke into a smile and looked at his unexpected visitor. "Danny-man," he said "what can I do for you buddy?"

Danny never showed much expression on his face but this time was different. He looked sad.

Tony saw the look, got concerned and invited him into his room. Danny entered the room grabbing something from beside the outer doorframe that Tony hadn't seen. It was a set of golf clubs. He walked into Tony's room, moved over to a stuffed chair that was in the corner and seated himself with the clubs beside him.

"Can we talk privately, Tony?" Danny said in a low voice.

Tony could see the serious look in his eyes so he closed the door and went back over to his bed and sat down.

"Sure Danny, what's wrong?" he asked. Tony was concerned now. He wanted to help his friend no matter what. Danny hadn't said anything more so Tony was looking at him, quietly trying to guess what was going on. His eyes were drawn to the golf clubs and questions swirled around in his head.

"Did he want to play golf?" Tony thought. He had never seen Danny swing a club in all the time he had been there. He had never seen Danny out on the diamond when he and Floyd were practicing.

Tony could tell a great set of clubs from a cheap one and these were top quality. They were "Pings, Golden Masters" that shone like polished pieces of silver. The fog started to clear and Tony recognized the clubs. These beautiful clubs belonged to Floyd Finn!

More questions boiled up in Tony's mind, but before he could raise them, Danny broke his silence.

"He liked you Tony, he really liked you. He told me that many times. He talked about what a good serviceman you were becoming and how you loved the game of golf. He wanted you to have these."

With that, Danny handed the clubs over to Tony who was still sitting on his bed in shock.

"What the hell is going on?" was all Tony could manage.

With that Danny leaned forward and said "he's drinking again, Tony and has been for a long time." Danny went on to say that after the shit show in the Ranks Club, Floyd and Angy had a big fight, Floyd came back to the barracks for awhile. Word got back to Floyd that Angy had been seen in The Stockman's bar partying with a lot of guys.

This pissed Floyd right off and that night he drove down to the motel he had put her up in and went in to confront her. She wasn't there. What Floyd saw struck him like a lightning bolt.

There on the little table by the window sat his conscience bottle of Crown Royal, open, half empty and two glasses!

Tony could envision Floyd's world crashing in around him as he fell off the edge of sobriety into the darkness.

He envisioned Floyd grabbing the bottle and pulling it to his lips, feeling the burn of the alcohol as it ran down his throat. At first he would want to puke and then an old familiar warm feeling would come over him. The bottle was empty in three pulls.

Danny went on to say that Floyd then drove to The Stockman's bar and burst into the main hall looking for her, but had no luck. He went to the bar and threw back two whiskies, bolted to the door and headed for The Leonard Bar just down the street.

He opened the front door with enough force to slam it back on its hinges but the place was so noisy, no one noticed. Through his blurred vision and alcohol haze, Floyd saw Angy sitting on a native motorcycle gang leader's lap. She was laughing loudly while his hands moved all over her.

Floyd screamed at her and called her a whore and as he moved toward them the lights went out and he woke on the floor of the drunk-tank at the local Police Station. His eyes were swollen and he had numerous cuts and bruises around his head and face. His clothes were torn beyond recognition and he was missing a shoe. Floyd found out later that he had been beaten by three members of the motorcycle gang and thrown into the alley even before he got close to Angy.

Danny went on to say that Floyd wasn't around much anymore but he had been seen downtown a time or two, sitting by himself in a bar, totally drunk.

Danny rose from the chair, said he was sorry about Floyd and left the room.

Tony sat there looking at the clubs and shaking his head. A lot had gone on while he had been away in Edmonton.

Chapter 10

Things moved quickly over the next couple of months. Tony went out on courses he needed to advance, and did. He was given more responsibility and at times even mentored new Privates as they arrived on-site.

He bought another car, a new Honda Civic that he really liked and could go weeks on one tank of gas. This Tony really appreciated because gas was 57 cents a gallon!

His time at Kamloops was coming to an end and Tony was advised that he was to be transferred soon to another Radar Site in Labrador, called "Goose Bay." He was told that he would be leaving in two weeks and would be given another two weeks to travel across Canada and that included taking a ferry up to Goose Bay which would take three of those days.

Tony did some research on his new posting. Goose Bay Radar Site and airport were built in 1941 and had the longest military runway in the north east. Also, it was the alternate landing site for the NASA Space Shuttle!

The Radar Site itself had been built in 1964, on the same site that the old Radar Site was and could still be accessed by many doors around the new Site.

Tony knew that this was an "isolated" posting and things he now took for granted were not going to be available, but he was ready for the adventure.

He had decided to stop in Port Nichols on the way east, for a short stay. He would say hello to old friends and show them that he was doing fine.

Two weeks came and went and after all the goodbyes were said, Tony found himself packed, ready to go and drove through the main gate for the last time.

He could see all this great stuff in front of him and wondered where he'd be in 10 years. One thing was for sure, he would never forget his first posting.

Tony didn't know it at the time but three years later The Leonard Hotel would burn to the ground mysteriously and eleven years after that, Kamloops Base would close its gates for good and be abandoned only to live again for a short period of time in 1990 as the Hollywood movie "Cadence" was made there, starring "Charlie Sheen."

Chapter 11

Tony liked to drive, and this trip across Canada was going to be relaxing and exciting all at once. It had been some time since his accident in the snow covered mountains. It was spring now and the roads were clear. He promised himself that he would stop and look around as he headed east for Calgary which was his first stop.

He loved driving in the mountains; it was hard to figure out just how the men back then had carved the roads and tunnels that were used now. One thing was for sure; there was always construction and a lot of trucks.

The day was moving right along and the Honda was making good time. Calgary was just ahead and Tony checked into a road-side hotel and grabbed a beer.

While sitting at the bar he thought of all that had happened in Kamloops and what he would be doing in Goose Bay; all that was ahead of him. Once back on the road the next morning, the terrain changed after Calgary. He left the mountains and headed into the rolling hills and then into the flat lands of the prairies.

Tony thought to himself that driving in Saskatchewan was like driving on the moon. There was nothing but miles and miles of flat farmland and a road so straight it was hard at times to believe you were moving.

A few days into the trip and Tony could see Winnipeg and then Thunder Bay in his rearview mirror as the terrain changed again. This time the road was carved into the dense forests of pine trees and rock-faced walls. The big thing here was the fact that there was no radio reception so Tony was quite happy to listen to his vast collection of music like CCR, Led Zeppelin, Leonard Skinner or Cat Stevens on his 8-track, and let the miles roll away.

After what seemed to be an eternity, and a journey that didn't want to end, Tony popped out of the forest to see a huge lake in front of him. Lake Superior was the largest body of water in the five lake chain and all Tony had to do was keep the water on his right side, which seemed like forever. He would eventually be in Sault Ste Marie.

Passing through the Sault was very difficult. It was the main transportation hub and every truck in the country was there at the same time. Slowly, Tony headed to the east side of the city and finally saw the first sign for Niagara Falls and

Toronto. He had been on the road for several days now and he was looking forward to a break.

It was late and Tony wanted to be fresh for the next day so he pulled into a Super 8. There was a restaurant with a small bar attached, so it seemed to be a no-brainer. He would have a light supper, a drink at the bar and call it a night.

Restaurant food isn't great food so Tony finished his supper without really knowing what he had ordered and strolled into the small lounge, sat at the bar, and ordered a rum and coke.

He glanced around the room to see that it wasn't really full but there were other people there, travellers mostly he guessed. At the other end of the bar a couple sat deep in discussion about something or other. Tony didn't pay too much attention other than the guy seemed to be really agitated about something and was trying to get the young lady's attention so she would listen to him.

Not his business, Tony turned around and ordered another drink. A half hour went by and because the lounge was fairly quiet, Tony was inadvertently catching parts of the conversation from the far side of the bar.

"It's a mistake Donna," the stranger said. "I don't want you to do it. I won't let you do it. I've known you forever and I won't let you throw your life away."

Tony was interested now. Things were heating up. The young lady was holding her own.

"It's my decision Gary, it's made. There's nothing here that can keep me in this shitty little town."

Gary's voice got louder; "but why the military, Donna? You're never going to make it, you'll fail and you'll be back here begging me to take you back. They're just a bunch of monkeys marching around and doing what they're told. Is that what you want?"

Gary was standing up now, looking down at her and pounding his finger on the bar.

Tony took a deep breath, rose up from his chair and slowly made his way to the other end of the bar. He didn't like being called a monkey and he was going to educate this shitty little civilian.

He sat down next to Donna and ordered another drink. Gary was looking at him with disgust and was puffing out his chest in protest. Tony wasn't even looking at him but he knew Gary's type.

"Sit down and shut up man, you're not scaring anybody."

Gary was so shocked that his jaw opened and he sat down, staring at the stranger that had invaded his world.

Tony finally turned to the lady and really saw her for the first time. Quite attractive was his first impression, around 5 foot something with light brown hair to her shoulder and deep blue eyes.

Tony could see that Gary was getting to her by the tear in her eye and quivering lip. He slowly took out his wallet and removed a card from its holder, putting it down in front of her.

Gary came alive and started to mouth off. "Who the fuck do you think you are, and what….." That was as far as he got.

Tony rose and looked at Gary with dark death in his eyes. "If you open your mouth one more time, I'm going to beat you to the ground, and that's a promise," Tony whispered.

Gary went silent again as Tony sat down and looked at this beauty beside him. She was looking at the card in front of her with wide eyes.

"Is this what I think it is?" she asked.

"That's my military identification card, I'm in the military. My name is Tony and I'm not a monkey."

He then looked right at Gary who was melting in his chair.

Donna held the card like it was a rare manuscript.

Tony asked her the next couple of questions all the while looking at Gary, daring him to talk.

"When did you sign up and when do you leave?" he asked.

She smiled and told him she had signed the line the month before and was leaving in two weeks. Donna said she was going to be a supply technician and travel all over the world.

They talked for hours about the military and how it had affected Tony's life. He told her about the horror of boot camp and the satisfaction of succeeding and having a career.

Gary just sat there staring holes into Tony's soul. He hated Tony, but what could he do?

Donna hung onto every word and knew she had made the right decision.

It was getting late and Tony knew he still had a long way to go, so he said goodnight to Donna and hoped to see her down the line.

He got up to leave and stopped to look at Gary one more time. "You know you're an asshole, don't you?" he asked. "If I ever hear you calling military members monkeys again, I will be your worst nightmare." Tony then left the lounge and went to his room.

The day had been long and was catching up with him quickly. The room was dark and the bed was really not that bad. Tony was asleep in minutes, but he came full awake in the middle of the night to what he thought was a light knocking.

"What the hell is this about?" he thought. He moved to the door, thinking it must be housekeeping since he had left a wakeup call. He opened the door a crack to find Donna standing there with tears in her eyes.

"We had a terrible fight after you left and he walked out on me calling me all kinds of names."

Tony opened the door full and Donna fell into his arms, sobbing and holding him tightly. He closed the door and they kissed deeply.

The rest of the night was warm and necessary for both of them. They fell asleep in each other's arms and Tony didn't hear a thing until the wake-up call came. He rolled over and she was already gone, like she was never there except for the memory.

.

Chapter 12

Tony was on the road again, before the heavy traffic set in so he was able to make good time. Before long, Toronto came into view and Tony started to see things he remembered from back in the dark days. He came off the Trans Canada and onto the QEW. Memories of Junior and the wake came flooding back and he knew this blacktop would bring him back to Port Nichols and the memories that waited for him there.

He pulled into a Howard Johnson just on the outskirts of Port Nichols, registered and had lunch before setting himself a plan of action. He was only going to be spending a few days here and he still had a way to go before he was to see his sister in Newfoundland and finally get on the ferry for the three day run up to Goose Bay Labrador.

Liz and Mo were his first call and as he drove up to the rooming house and got out of the car, he could hear a squeal from the kitchen window and Liz came crashing out the door on the run. She slammed into him, squeezing him tightly.

She smelled of coffee and baking. "Welcome back Tony! You've been missed," she sighed. Tony let her go, stood back, and took a better look at Liz for the first time. She still looked like Miss Kitty from "Gunsmoke" but had added a few more lines. She looked great.

She hurried him into the house and sat him at the table, in a seat he knew well. She gave him coffee and a fresh cinnamon bun before sitting back to stare at him for a while. "You look great Tony; life in the military is treating you well. Are you happy? Do you need anything? Why are you here?" she asked.

Before he could answer any of her questions, Liz shouted down the hall. "Mo! We have company!"

A door opened somewhere down the hall and Tony could hear his old friend moving toward the kitchen. Before Mo got there he yelled "who is it Liz Darlin?" Mo stopped in his tracks and a big smile broke out on his face. He moved forward and wrapped his big arms around his friend and squeezed.

Tony didn't think Mo was ever going to let him loose, but he'd be needing air shortly so he hoped soon.

"What are you doing here boy? Are you hurt? Sure is good to see you," Mo beamed.

Tony sat them both down and explained that he was passing through on his way to Labrador, his next posting. He told them how much he loved being in the military and that he was a Corporal now. He told them about the accident and the pastor.

Mo stopped him and was about to give him shit for not calling but Liz put her hand on his arm and he calmed down. They both agreed that Tony looked happy and well. They had missed him dearly since he last left.

Liz told Tony that Mo had quit working at the bar two years back. It was getting just too dangerous even for him. He was a permanent fixture at Liz's now and quite the handyman around the place.

Tony could see that Mo was holding her hand as she spoke and put her head on his shoulder.

Tony told them that he was going to see Olive before he left and then he'd have to get moving. He had a long way to travel and a ferry to catch. He promised to call when he got to his new Site and stay closer in touch with them.

He spent the rest of the day with Liz and Mo. It was like he had never left, but the sun started to go down and he had to get going.

Tears from Liz and bear hugs from Mo got him out the door before they could see the emotion he was feeling inside surface.

Back at the Hotel he settled in for the night, thinking about how lucky he was to have such friends in his life. Tomorrow he would go over to Olive's and then be on his way the following day.

He had decided not to see if he could find the old man, chances were that he wasn't in that house anymore anyway and Tony didn't need the hassle.

Up early, breakfast and out the door put Tony on Hastings Street heading down to Olive's townhouse. He passed things he remembered, bringing up good memories and bad.

He turned down Olive's street, knowing that she'd be out on the front steps with her cup of tea. Sure enough there she was.

Olive didn't recognize him right away or the car either; so she was wary as he pulled up to the front of the house. He stepped out of the car and her eyes lit up. She smiled a big smile, raised her small frail body and held out her arms to embrace him as he came near. "Didn't think I'd see you again boy," she said.

Tony thought she would hug him forever, but eventually she stepped back and asked him "did you eat? How about a cup of Earl Grey? What are you doing here? How long can you stay?"

She had plenty of questions just like Liz.

Tony answered the best he could. He told her that he'd be leaving the next morning, but had to stop and see her before heading east. He looked around and asked about the girls. Olive told him that the girls had all grown up and moved out on their own. They visited often and that was enough for her.

She could see that Tony was avoiding the big question so she answered his silent stare. "He went bad Tony," she said. "Mark's fully patched now and meaner than a junk yard dog." She lowered her head then, so Tony couldn't see her face. "After you left he spent all of his time with Skip and the club. He didn't bother coming around here except to borrow money or sleep on the couch. His girlfriend left him soon after your last visit. He turned hard and cold and was making a reputation in town as Skip's head breaker and collector. Last time he was here he was high on something and wanted my rent money for more drugs."

Olive went on to tell Tony that she could see he was carrying a gun in his belt, but it didn't scare her. She told him to leave and never come back and Mark raised his hand like he was going to slap her. Olive said that she stood her ground and Mark backed down slamming the door behind him and breaking the glass as he left. That was the last time she saw him.

"Jesus Ma, I'm so sorry, is there anything I can do?"

Olive told him that she was ok and not to worry. She was a tough old bird.

They visited far into the evening but eventually Tony said he had to go because he wanted to be on the road early.

Olive hugged him warmly and touched his face. "You be careful and phone once in a while, just to let me know you're ok."

Tony said he would for sure and was out the door climbing into his car.

She stayed on the stoop until he was out of sight, turned and walked back in.

It was 8 PM and Tony was heading back to the Hotel when he decided to swing by the Franklin for one last look. He stopped at the light across from the bar waiting to move, when he noticed a cab across the intersection from him waiting too. The light turned green and Tony moved forward to meet and pass the cab in the middle of the intersection.

As the cab passed by Tony glanced at the driver and recognized him immediately. It was Dick!

Tony continued to move but stared holes into Dick's head. He was sure that Dick had not recognized him until the very last second before they passed each other. It was enough for him to know that the brief encounter with Dick would drive the old man crazy for years.

He rose early and was on the road. He still had five days to make the ferry, but he wanted to get there early so he could visit his sister. He hadn't seen her for over 12 years and during that time he had become an uncle three times.

He got back onto the Trans Canada once more and headed east again, up the lake head to Quebec and the St. Lawrence River. He spoke very little French but still figured he'd need one more tank of fuel to get through the province so he tanked up just before entering Quebec. He entered Montreal and immediately got lost trying to get across the Champlain Bridge.

Finally, after two tries he put the river on his left side and headed for New Brunswick.

The highway weaved through rolling hills again and masses of forests were on either side of the road.

Tony was rolling along, stopping when he needed and always waking early to be on the road again. Nova Scotia was getting close and he started to think of the last time he had seen his sister and the fact that they'd be together again. Once through Nova Scotia and after a short ferry ride from North Sydney to Port aux Basque he was finally in Newfoundland.

Chapter 13

The Cove where Sybil and her husband Randy lived was still a few hours away but Tony was sure he'd be there sometime that afternoon. He had made the trip up to Newfoundland in three days of long driving but this would give Tony two days to visit before boarding the Henderson Ferry for the three day cruise up to Goose Bay, Labrador.

Newfoundland, or the rock as it's called, was flat, forested and windy. The towns were few and far between with miles and miles of nothing on both sides of the road. There was one hazard that you had to watch for at all times and that was moose. They were everywhere and caused many accidents over the years by stepping out onto the road at anytime, day or night. If you hit a moose, you could easily die. They say it is like hitting a building at full speed.

Tony finally turned into a tiny Cove called "Mary's Arm." It was a fishing village with not much else there. There were maybe 50 small houses in various stages of repair, two churches, a small store and a fish plant with a large dock with numerous boats tied to it.

The nearest gas station was 30 miles away so the locals had a large fuel container located near the fish plant for emergency situations.

Tony knew his sister's house was right next to one of the churches and across the street from a graveyard. It wasn't hard to find.

He drove up to the driveway and she came running out of the house and nearly ripped him out of the car wrapping her arms around him and started to cry. They hugged each other for many minutes before letting go and looked at each other smiling.

It had been 12 years but to Tony she hadn't changed a bit. Sybil's smile turned to a frown and she slapped him lightly on the forehead and asked "what took you so long to visit?"

For the next two days Tony and Sybil talked each other's ears off. Tony told her about Dick, the motorcycle gang and why he was now in the military. Sybil told him about leaving Port Nichols with her now husband, Randy and returning to his family's home in Mary's Arm, raising a family and being very happy.

Randy showed Tony the fish plant and took him out on one of the boats to collect lobster. He got sick as a dog at first with the rolling motion, but still had a great day with his long lost brother-in-law.

His nieces were a handful and never stopped talking but Tony could see everybody was happy in the Cove.

Two days went quickly and it was time for Tony to get to the ferry which was two hours away in the Port of St. Anthony. He promised to call and visit more, seeing that they were only a ferry ride away.

Hugs, kisses and many tears later, he was on the road down to St. Anthony and his date with the Henderson.

Chapter 14

Tony was on schedule. It was May 31 and he didn't have to report in until the morning of June 4. This was another first for Tony, three days on a ferry and he had a state room. How hard could it be?

It had been quite a trip across Canada but now Tony was looking forward to the end of this adventure and a new one in Goose Bay. He pulled into St. Anthony with plenty of time to spare. He wasn't to board until 1000 hours and he still had an hour to look around before getting in line.

He had read that the Henderson was a newly commissioned ferry and this was to be her second run up to Goose Bay. She was as big as a city block and as Tony drove his tiny Honda Civic into the ferry's massive underbelly, he still couldn't see how this steal monster could stay afloat.

The weather had turned and the Atlantic was slamming up on the sea walls moving the huge vessel side to side as the winds got stronger.

Inside the belly of the beast Tony could see rows upon rows of new cars. He would find out later that Goose Bay had an Auto Dealership and these cars were this year's stock.

There were stacks of cargo and pallet upon pallet of beer along one side and heavy machinery in another area, for what Tony had no idea.

The Henderson was transporting supplies needed to operate the remote city of Goose Bay for half the year. Tony moved to the upper level and tried to take a walk around the massive ferry as it pulled out of the harbour, but the weather was worsening so he changed his mind. "Maybe later," he thought. He'd have a light lunch in the cafeteria and then into his state room to relax.

Later, while Tony was looking out onto the Atlantic, he was amazed that he could still see icebergs in the distance at this time of the year. Later he would find out the hard way that Goose Bay stayed pretty much near freezing all year long. It really only had two weeks or so of mild temperatures. One thing was for sure, the wind never stopped blowing.

Tony had a nervous night that kept him awake because of the high winds and swells as big as a house so he looked out the deck windows into the black water of the Atlantic.

He spent many hours the next day in the Arcade room and in the bar sipping rum and coke and listening to music. He got to talking to other passengers that were heading to Goose Bay also. There were a couple of military families onboard, but for the most part, the passengers were locals.

One of the passengers, John Munro, described Happy Valley, Labrador to Tony as a small town next to the military base where most of the locals worked in one form or another. He said that there wasn't much in the small town really, a Hudson's Bay Store, school house, a few small shops, a liquor store and a small RCMP Station which consisted of one car and three constables. He went on to say that there were only seven miles of road in Happy Valley that were useable but most of the time there was snow on the ground so the locals used snowmobiles.

The high point of the week was when the natives came into town from the reserves in an old school bus because it was welfare day!

John said they would shop in the Hudson's Bay store, go to Mary Brown's Chicken for lunch and then to the liquor store where they would sit outside and get drunk. Those that weren't arrested would get back on the bus at the end of the day and leave town.

Tony was shaking his head at this, he could hardly wait!

Two days out, and heading north Tony was watching the shoreline change from trees to grey rock from the covered observation deck. He knew he was getting close. It was colder now and the water looked dark, cold and rough. The trip had been awesome and scary at the same time but he was tired of it and just wanted to get there. There were only so many things you could do on a ferry and Tony was already tired of them all.

He decided to make it an early night; he would read a little and start fresh the next morning. It was the last night on the ferry and he wanted to be fresh when Goose Bay came into view.

He closed his eyes and drifted off only to be startled awake by the ship's intercom system coming alive. "All passengers and crew are to report to their life boat stations and prepare to abandon ship!"

"Was he hearing this correctly?" The P.A. repeated it again and again and seemed to be getting louder. Tony was mildly annoyed. He thought it was probably a lifeboat drill. "What the hell time is it?" he said to himself, "so much for a good night's sleep."

He grabbed his coat and life vest and reported to his boat station as ordered, out on the wet rolling deck in the middle of the night. He told himself that he was going to voice his opinion about this shit as soon as it was over.

It was really dark out, except for when the massive search lights moved over the ferry and out into the black as the huge ferry pitched badly.

The crew was moving around just a little too quickly for his liking and no one was apologizing for the disturbance. The crew was serious and deliberate, keeping the passengers in line and getting the boats over the side.

The massive ferry's horns started to call out into the dark and suddenly flares were being ignited and rocketed into the night sky to explode into massive stars several hundred feet into the air.

This got Tony's attention and panic started to well up in his chest; "THIS WASN'T A DRILL! This ship was really going down! What the hell happened?" he asked himself.

The wind was whipping at his face and trying to take the life jacket off his back.

He didn't hear an explosion or feel the ferry slam into anything, but here he was. It was 2 o'clock in the morning and Tony wondered who in hell was driving the boat? He could feel the sweat on his back and more water running down his neck. More panic set in. "Am I going to die tonight?"

Tony's mind was playing tricks on him and he started rubbing his hands intently.

Suddenly a crew member was in his face, staring right at him and using a calm, stern voice he said "sir, please move forward and get into the boat, now!"

Tony didn't hesitate. He got into the life boat the best he could and almost fell over the side with all the rocking motion of the ferry. He seated himself near the back, near the motor and rudder. A crewman entered the boat and took a seat next to Tony. He checked the engine and started it.

The command was given to lower their lifeboat, slamming it into the side of the bulkhead and in seconds Tony was bobbing up and down like a cork in the black Atlantic Ocean in the middle of the night.

The horns still blared and the rockets lit up the night, but Tony could see clearly that there was something terribly wrong with the ferry. It was listing to the front and the left side and was taking on water quickly. He could see the lights of a dozen or so life boats bobbing in the dark, moving quickly away from the ferry to safety. She was going down!

"Why in hell was she sinking?" Tony thought. He was so fixated on the horror that filled his view that he didn't notice that the crewman driving his lifeboat was making his way to a tiny light in the distance that he could barely see in the darkness.

Tony looked around now and saw that all twelve boats were moving in the same direction, the tiny little light in the darkness. He knew he was only a few hundred yards from the coastline because they had been following it north since they left St. Anthony, but where was the shore in the dark? There was only the tiny little light.

Tony looked back at the crippled ferry. Her bow was completely under water now, and the stern was high in the air. Some of the lights were still working on her deck and the ferry's silhouette in the dark was eerie. He looked again at the light in the distance on shore. It was getting closer and he thought he could make out what looked like a small lighthouse.

At first he thought he wasn't going to survive this night but hope began to creep back into his bones and he became keenly aware that he was cold and damp. They had given him a blanket when he got into the lifeboat, but that was little protection against the cold Atlantic winds.

He then became aware of the sound of waves breaking on the shoreline and minutes later he could see land. He was going to make it!

Chapter 15

The boats hit the beach and everyone piled out to pull them higher onto land. Tony looked back out into the ocean and saw the stern of the ferry slip silently under the water. He could see that some of the lights were still working before everything went black.

He became keenly aware of the waves crashing on the shore and the seagulls screaming at them in the night through the wind and rain. "Where the hell are we?" he thought to himself. Flashlights came on and the Captain and crewmen gathered the passengers around them.

"We're safe," the Captain said over the sound of the waves. "This island is called 'Black Tickle.' No one lives here but there is an automatic light beacon as you can see. We radioed our position to Marine Search and Rescue in Gander before abandoning the ship and they are currently moving to our location with air support to get us back to Gander. We should see helicopters shortly after dawn. That means we're here for the rest of the night, folks. Let's make some fires and get some coffee brewing to take the night chill away. We have rations in our ready bags if you're hungry. It's going to be a long wet night, so try and get some rest if you can."

Tony was sitting on a rock looking out at the ocean to where the ferry had been. He knew he had dodged another bullet this night, just as he had done before on that fateful day in the snow.

He was sitting there quietly feeling the warmth of the fire and realizing just how great a cup of coffee can really be then he snapped back to reality and to the present. "Damn" he said, shaking his head, "I've lost another car!"

The next morning Tony, the passengers and crew members watched three large Chinook Helicopters come over the horizon and head straight for them. Three hours of flying time later they were in Gander at the Rescue Centre having hot food and coffee and being attended to by military medical personnel for stress and trauma.

A C130 Transport plane had been dispatched from Goose Bay during the night to Gander. The C130 would fly the passengers back to Goose Bay instead of taking another ferry.

When they finally arrived in Goose Bay, Tony was greeted by a fierce north wind and blowing sand as he exited the tail of the aircraft and everyone was again taken to a medical inspection room to be cleared before release.

Tony and two other service members were taken to the Headquarters building where they met the Base Commander who warmly welcomed them to Goose Bay.

Tony was given a room in a very old barracks that housed 25 other men and he was advised that he would be receiving new uniforms the next day, but his civilian clothes were his responsibility. He would be compensated for his loss, but for right now, what he was wearing was all he had.

Tony realized he had not slept in 24 hours so bed was the best thing to do.

The next morning he was taken to stores and had new uniforms issued along with a much warmer coat. He found the Mess Hall and was quietly eating his lunch alone when a tall, thin Sergeant and a much shorter Master Corporal came up to his table and sat down.

"Corporal Simons, my name is Bond and this here is your new Crew Chief, Master Corporal Townsend. We were to meet you at the dock and screech you in properly but we heard that the ferry went down and is now part of a new reef and you spent the night on 'The Tickle.' No matter what you're thinking about this place right now, it's not all that bad. It tends to grow on you. We're glad you're here, we can use the help."

Tony was given the rest of the day off and Master Corporal Townsend, Jerry, took him around the Base, hangar line and finally the Radar Site which was to be his home for the next two years.

The DMCC looked the same as Kamloops but the screens had a larger presentation of the Atlantic Ocean on them as they reached out to the north and east. Their job was to watch for Russian Aircraft coming in from the north.

Jerry then drove Tony into the town of Happy Valley. He showed him around the various stores and buildings that had been there even before the Base was built. They were very old and looked it. Jerry explained about the local natives and when they were expected in town. He told Tony about the time the RCMP had locked the local Native Chief up for drinking in public and the whole tribe attacked the tiny police station trying to get him out.

The RCMP was barricaded in the Police Station and the natives turned over the cruiser and set it on fire. The RCMP finally relented and let the Chief go.

"Never a dull moment in the Goose, Tony," Jerry said, "never."

Chapter 16

Tony took to his new Site right away. The work was the same, but different. There were new people and new surroundings, but to Tony, it was all about the experience. It was exciting watching Russian Aircraft on the screens and Canadian Fighters rushing toward them to intercept and demand that they leave the airspace.

He even liked the switchboard now because everyone on the Goose used the military switchboard to call their relatives for free during the silent hours around midnight.

The best times were in the middle of the night when the main switchboard operator, Cora, in Happy Valley let Tony listen to the pervs, sickos and creepy people that would phone her to harass her and use filthy language or proposition her.

Tony finally met Cora one night when she was in the Junior Ranks Club with a few of her friends. Tony had just started working at the bar in his free time and someone happened to yell out "hey Tony!"

Cora's ears perked up and she had to go over to the bar to ask the young man there if he was the same Tony who worked the switchboard. The funny thing was that the operator that handled the switchboard at night was a tiny 65 year old woman with a sense of humour and who was missing some teeth.

Tony shook her hand and they had a good laugh at all the stuff that was going on behind the switchboard late at night.

Tony had other duties; one of them was doing security rounds with a flash light in the old original barracks under which the new Radar Site had been built.

This area was complete with World War II bunks, kitchen and common areas. It looked to Tony like they just got up and walked away. There were magazines on tables, pictures on the walls and pots in the kitchen area ready to go. It was a little unnerving for Tony, walking in this area in the middle of the night with nothing but a flashlight, listening to the wind howl just outside the windows.

Birds had gotten in somehow and would scare the hell out of you when they flew pass your face in the dark. There were noises, always noises.

Goose Bay was constantly cold. The winters were ten months long and in an isolated area, you feel it more. It isn't like you can go down to the corner store and buy a coke or go see a movie. Everything is flown in or ferried in, and the ferry didn't run in the winter.

To make things worse, when Tony's ferry sank, so did all the beer that was in her hold. It made for a very long winter when all there was to drink was skunky ten penny beer.

Everyone did anything they could to stay busy and Tony was no exception. He ran a lapidary shop; was the bartender for two messes and joined the short-wave radio club just to talk to new people.

The topper was that TV shut down at 2100 hours in Labrador, so there better be movies to watch, even if you've watched them over and over again.

What the Goose lacked in amenities, it made up in military bars. There were five different bars in a one mile area; two were Canadian, one American, one British and an open bar for all ranks.

You could stay drunk in Goose Bay 24 hours a day, if you wanted to. Everyone had a favourite bar and Tony's was the British Bulldog Club. It was a great place to party all the time. The local women loved to frequent it as well.

Every weekend the place was packed with ladies from all over the Labrador area. They even flew in just to party at the Bulldog.

This is where Tony met Gloria.

Chapter 17

One Friday night, Tony was at the Bulldog. The place was packed as always and he was trying to get to the bar. He wasn't really looking around, but out of the corner of his eye he noticed a group of girls off by themselves. They were laughing and drinking some kind of shots.

They seemed to be having a great time fending off guys hitting on them, when one of the ladies in the group got up and headed for the door.

Tony was definitely interested in this lady so he followed her out to the parking lot. He stopped her and asked if she needed any help. She said her name was Gloria and she was waiting for a cab. She had had enough of the club and was heading home.

The cab was really late and Tony and Gloria, while standing in the parking lot, struck up an immediate friendship that would last for the remainder of Tony's time in Goose Bay.

It wasn't long after meeting her that Tony learned that his good friend Keith had been posted to North Bay and wasn't really happy. Tony was aware that a C130 made regular flights to Trenton and it was always possible to hitch a ride and from there it was only a short distance by train in the bar car that would put him in North Bay before last call at the Junior Ranks Mess.

So it was that Tony spent most of his time with Gloria in Goose Bay but whenever their schedules lined up, he would head to North Bay to spend a few days with his old friend.

When they were together, Tony and Keith would talk about the military and what was ahead for them. Both agreed they just didn't know.

Tony told Keith about Gloria and how their relationship was growing. Shortly after they had first met, Gloria had told Tony she had been married before and had three small children. She was divorced and living with her parents in Happy Valley and working in the kitchen on the Base.

Keith listened quietly and finally asked Tony where he thought the relationship was going. He hesitated for a minute and answered. "I am very happy being with Gloria."

When they were together Tony felt that things couldn't be better but the built-in family thing bothered him. He hadn't said anything to her.

Tony went back to North Bay a few more times to give his friend support. He knew Keith was looking for a way out of the military.

Chapter 18

Tony's time in the Goose was coming to an end and he knew he would be posted soon. He had to decide whether or not to bring his relationship with Gloria to another level. He had to make the decision soon.

His posting finally came in, Great Falls, Montana in 30 days! He was happy and torn all at the same time. He knew he had to tell Gloria.

They met for coffee at the CANEX that afternoon and Tony told her he was leaving soon.

Tears welled up in her eyes and she could barely speak. "Are you taking me and the kids with you, Tony? You said you loved me Tony. You can't just leave us here."

She waited for his answer, not breathing then it came—

"I can't marry you, Gloria. I'm barely able to look after myself let alone a full family."

Reality was setting in. She was not going with him and he wouldn't be staying with her. She would be alone again. She finally exhaled and sat bolt upright in her chair wiping tears from her cheeks.

The silence between them seemed to last forever. Finally, she got up and looked down at him, picked up her coke and threw it in his face. "You're a son of a bitch, Tony." Then she turned and walked away.

As sad as it was, Tony had to get his head in the game. He would miss Gloria terribly, but it was just too much responsibility too soon.

First things first, he needed a car!

Chapter 19

Goose Bay was so small he hadn't needed a car up until then. There were only seven miles of road and they were covered with snow most of the year.

He got a ride from a friend to Happy Valley, to the only car dealership within a couple thousand miles. "Honest Ernie's New and Used Cars" the sign said. "Great deals every day" the sign said.

Tony was skeptical. The Goose was isolated, everything was expensive. A bag of recombined milk sold for over $4 if you could find it.

He wasn't on the lot five seconds when Honest Ernie himself came bounding out of his trailer with out-stretched hand.

He was a tall, thin, nervous looking man with sweaty palms and a painted on smile. Tony had been scanning the little lot as Ernie began to rattle off his spiel. "Best prices anywhere," Ernie jabbered. "Glad to help a serviceman. Had dinner just the other day on the Base with a couple I sold a car to. Nice people, really. What are you looking for young fellow?" Ernie probed.

Tony silently continued looking over the small lot. There were trucks mostly of varying ages and condition, small cars and even a couple of jeeps. That was not what caught Tony's eye. There in the corner, slightly out of view, was what he was looking for. It was a 1978 Chevy Caprice Classic Coupe, dark blue and because it was only a year old, had low mileage.

Tony knew this ride was what he was looking for. Ernie knew it too and tried to hard sell him into paying the list price, $5700. After haggling back and forth for about a half an hour Tony showed Ernie $4900 and threatened to walk off the lot.

Ernie snatched the money and handed over the keys. Tony had his ride!

Less than thirty days later he was on his way to Great Falls Montana, alone.

Chapter 20

This time the ferry ride was uneventful and Tony sat back and enjoyed the trip. He had decided the night before to change his travel plans and visit a friend from his past that had never been too far from his thoughts.

Betty lived just outside Pennsylvania and he warmed at the thought of seeing her again.

Once Tony arrived in Newfoundland he spent a day visiting his sister in the Cove and marveled at how big the girls had grown in just two years.

The next day he drove away and arrived in Port aux Basques. This time instead of booking passage to North Sydney, he paid for a one way ticket to Bar Harbor, Maine on a different ferry.

It was going to take 18 hours to make the crossing so Tony didn't bother with a berth. A club chair would do just fine.

Half way through the trip he became aware they were in the United States because they opened the casino and everyone gravitated there and began gambling.

He arrived in Bar Harbor very late that night and it was pissing down rain and windy as hell. He wasn't tired so he drove for a few more hours until it was time to pull over at a roadside hotel to sleep. Tomorrow he would see Betty and a warm feeling came over him as he drifted off.

Very early the next day he was on the road again. The drive to Pennsylvania was an easy couple of hours and would put Tony in Springside just after lunch.

As he passed the city limit's sign his heart began to race. It had been a long time, but she had never really been out of his thoughts.

He drove passed the Harpy's Motorcycle Club and wondered if it had changed much. Was Pierre Ledoux still the President? His memories of driving up to that gate on his Sportster with Mark next to him came rushing back.

He blinked, brought himself back to the present and drove on.

Betty's place was just 10 minutes away. It had been six years, but he remembered the way with little effort. The

Hardware Store was, as he had seen it last. There was no change.

He pulled up around back, parked and looked up at the upper apartment. Without waiting another second he ran up the stairs and knocked on the door, his heart racing on. "Would she be glad to see him?" he thought. "Would she fall into his arms and weep tears of happiness?"

Moments later the door opened and Tony's heart fell. It wasn't his Betty that answered, but an elderly lady with questioning eyes. "Can I help you young man?" she asked.

Tony was lost for words but managed to smile back at her and ask. "I'm sorry to bother you ma'am, but I was looking for a young woman that I thought lived here."

The old woman looked back at him and said "I've lived here alone these past three years and don't recall a young woman here before me. I'm sorry." Then she closed the door.

Tony stood there staring at the door, a million things racing through his mind. "Three years?" he questioned. "She's been gone three years! Holy Christ!" he thought and slowly climbed down the stairs.

He got back in his car to sit there and stare into nothing. Then a light came on in the dark panic he was feeling. "The shop!" jumped out at him. "Was she still working at the detail shop with her partner, T.L.?" It was a long shot, but Tony had nothing left to try. If she wasn't there, he'd have to forget her and move on.

The first thing he noticed as he pulled up to the shop was that it was bigger than he remembered. It seemed that they had expanded and the place looked professional. He walked through the door that activated a small bell announcing customers and waited.

The shop looked great. There was a comfortable waiting area and beautiful drawings on the wall. He recognized one of them in particular and smiled.

He had his back to the counter when he heard a voice behind him "can I help you?" the voice said. Tony turned around and his world stopped for a second as he recognized Betty right away even though she had her hair tied back and had paint smears on her forehead and cheek. To Tony she was captivating.

It took a full two seconds for Betty to come to terms with herself that Tony was indeed standing in front of her. She came around the counter and they fell into each others' arms, lost in the moment.

"Where have you been?" she sighed.

They broke apart but were still holding onto each other as Tony looked at her and confessed. "Growing up Betts, I had to grow up."

They both sat down on the waiting room couch and took each other in. Betty shook her head a little and spoke first. "I heard what happened with you and the club. Word got around quickly. They said you were disloyal and how Skip had taken your bike and threw you out."

"It didn't go down like that, Betty," Tony was shaking his head. "I had to make better choices for myself and Skip didn't like them." Tony paused "I joined the military and that's where I've been this last six years. I'm on my way to Montana right now. I'm posted there for two years. I was working up at Goose Bay, Labrador and they wanted me in Montana, so here I am."

Tony reached for her hand. "I couldn't drive by and not stop. By the way, did I mention you look spectacular and I'm very happy to see you again?"

Betty slowly pulled her hand away, paused a moment, looked at him fondly and began. "I thought of you often Tony, I really did. I was sad when I heard the news and wondered where you were for the longest time. I then buried myself in my work to keep from wondering and before I knew it, a year had gone by and then two and then more. My work was everything and in time I finally was able to put you in my past."

Tony could feel the pain of what was coming.

"I met someone Tony" she confessed. "He's a nice person and treats me well. We've been together for three years now and are talking about a future together."

Tony was dying inside but he didn't let it show. She had moved on as he had. He had no right to expect that she would be waiting for him. "I'm happy for you Betty," Tony smiled. "You deserve the best and it sounds like you have it."

They talked for an hour or so and Tony finally said he had to go and rose from the couch. "I'm glad I stopped, Betty," he said with a smile.

Betty hugged him and told him not to be a stranger. He hugged her again and left the shop without looking back.

As he drove away he knew that stopping had been the right thing to do. He could move on now.

Chapter 21

The rest of the trip across the Midwest was uneventful and Tony rolled into Great Falls in the middle of the night. His sponsor, Corporal Danny Wicks, was single and in his 20's with glasses and fiery red curly hair. He met Tony for breakfast the next morning and toured him around the Base for most of the day, making sure he had a room assigned and a meal card to eat with.

They toured the complex and Tony was surprised to see that it mirrored North Bay quite closely. He was informed that he would be working with Danny on "A Crew" the following night and that suited Tony just fine.

They hit it off right away and before long Tony was feeling right at home in his new posting. He still worried about his buddy in North Bay and how he was holding up.

A few months went along with no word from Keith until one fateful morning Tony finally got a call from him. He could tell Keith was excited and had trouble getting his news out in one breath.

"Tony, buddy," he said "I'm leaving the military and taking a job with a meteorological systems group out of Denver, working in the north on weather stations."

"Where the hell did that come from?" Tony asked. They talked off and on for most of the day and what came out of the conversation was that Tony would follow his friend. He would release from the military and join Keith in Winnipeg in a couple of weeks. They would then both fly down to Denver together.

It was obvious to Tony that his friend needed him so the choice was easy, but in the back of his mind a tiny warning signal was going off which he dismissed as nerves.

A week later, Tony was in Calgary, Alberta finishing his release paperwork and heading for Winnipeg the next day. He phoned Keith and told him he was on his way to Winnipeg and would see him there in a few days.

Keith told him he was just finishing up and would see him there soon.

"A new adventure," Tony thought to himself, "who would have guessed it?"

That would be the last time Tony heard from Keith for four months.

Chapter 22

Tony waited in Winnipeg that week and tried to contact Keith, but to no avail. No one knew where he was. He was just gone.

He had to report to the training centre in Denver in 30 days so he stayed busy by taking a bartender's job at a local sports bar. Still there was no sign of Keith.

Tony was getting pissed but he convinced himself that Keith would show up in Denver and explain.

That didn't happen. Thirty days later he was in Denver and the training began without Keith. Tony started to remember what he had given up to be with his friend. His entire career was trashed and now Keith was not there. Tony was enraged and it consumed him finally costing him the meteorological opportunity. He failed the training!

With Denver now in the toilet, he had to make some new plans. He decided to leave Denver and fly back to

Winnipeg since that was where his car was stored. He made a promise to himself that he would find his ex best friend and beat the shit out of him because it was his fault!

Chapter 23

It was midnight and snowing in Winnipeg when Tony landed and he had to wait until the next day to get his car out of storage. The Chevy Caprice that he had bought in Goose Bay had a few miles on it now but the engine was sound and the heater worked!

He remembered that Keith was originally from Saskatoon, Saskatchewan and that he had family there. He decided that he would start looking for him there.

Saskatoon was ten hours away but adrenalin made time and miles tick off quickly and before long he was there.

It was cold in Saskatoon and late in the afternoon. It had snowed the night before so the roads were shitty.

Tony took a room in a motel on 8th Street and vowed to begin his hunt in the morning. After a few beers and a sandwich he was back in his room looking out the window with determination in his eyes and fear nagging at him somewhere in the back of his mind.

"What had he done? Why had he not listened to that warning signal? He had blown his whole career. He had it made," he thought "and now he had nothing again. He only had a few bucks in his pocket and an old car that was on its last legs."

"Where was his old friend? Why didn't he show up in Denver?" A million other unanswered questions fuelled Tony's rage as he prepared to hunt Keith down. He needed a map and phone book, both easily obtained. The phonebook was in his room and the map he found at a nearby gas station.

He sat at the little table in his room and unfolded the map. He noticed right away the overall structure of the city. It was divided by a river and had at least five bridges connecting one side to the other. He noticed the legend said that the population was close to 150,000 people. The area around the city was mainly farming and mining.

He then opened the phone book to the "S's" looking for "Stoddard." He found six listings with that name and tried them all, asking to speak to Keith. Five came up short but on the last one there was a glimmer of light.

"Hello," said a voice on the phone.

Tony answered back "can I speak to Keith Stoddard please?"

The voice left the receiver and Tony could hear conversation in the background. "Ben, someone's looking for Keith," the voice said. "Who is it?" Ben asked. "He didn't say," the voice answered.

Ben took the receiver "who is this and what do you want?"

Tony could hear that the man on the phone was getting annoyed. "I'm looking for Keith Stoddard," Tony answered.

"What do you want him for?" Ben growled.

"My business," Tony growled back.

Ben's voice rose "Fuck off and don't call back!" then he slammed the receiver down.

Tony smiled to himself as he slowly put the receiver down, "so he is in town, now what?"

He remembered many conversations with Keith about the farm and his family and how hard it was for them. Ben drank a lot and Susan, his mother was always running away and coming back. His older sister, Marjorie, had married a Ukrainian farmer from the area and had three kids.

He was having trouble remembering her married name but he knew he would get it. He remembered it sounded like an animal's name. He started to rattle some off in his head. "Beaver, Muskrat, Woodchuck?" The light came on "Namche."

He moved to the phone book and fanned the pages to the "N's." To his surprise, there were twenty Namche's in the area. Tony thought to himself "this is a damn big family!"

He started making calls again and was getting nowhere until he got to the "L's." The phone rang and rang until a woman answered. Tony started the conversation calmer this time. "I'm looking for Keith Stoddard."

"Who is this?" Marjorie asked. "Why are you looking for him?"

"Just want to find him," Tony answered.

"He doesn't live here," she answered and hung up the phone.

He smiled to himself again, he had an address!

That evening, with his map in hand, he found Marjorie Namche's home address and parked outside for some time before going to the door and knocking.

He knew she had been watching from the window and was really quite surprised that she answered the door.

She was smaller than her brother, short blond hair and had a quick temper. "What do you want," she snapped. She knew it was the voice on the phone right away.

"I'm looking for Keith Stoddard," Tony said with no emotion in his voice and a dead stare.

"He doesn't live here," she said, her voice cracking.

Tony reached out and handed her a piece of paper. "This is my number; tell him I'm in town and looking for him."

She took the paper and slammed the door in his face before he had time to give her his name. He knew as he walked down the driveway to his car, she was already on the phone calling him; to warn him about this guy in town looking for him. Ben would have called him too.

Tony was getting into his room after having a burger and a beer next door. It was called the "Sport" something. The beer was cheap and the food not so bad. It would do for now.

It was coming up on 2000 hours and Tony was watching TV when the phone rang. "Hello," said the voice on the other end of the line. "Who the hell is this and why the hell are you looking for me?" Keith demanded.

"It's me, you asshole," Tony answered. "Where the hell have you been and what the hell are you doing here?" he growled on the phone. "You owe me an explanation, and it better be good, you bastard! I came all this way to lay a beating on you and I'm still a mind to."

Silence filled the air. Finally, Keith answered in a low voice. "Come over to the house tomorrow and I will explain." He gave Tony the address, which was, to his surprise, just down the street from the hotel Tony was staying at and a left onto Edwards Avenue.

Tony hung up the phone and stared into space. "It better be good," he said to himself.

Chapter 24

Tony headed out at 0800 hours the next morning. He drove up to and stopped in front of an old yellow house that had seen better days. It was small and needed paint badly. The trim was cracked and peeling away and the door had plywood over where a window had once been.

Tony guessed there was a dog because the bottom of the door was all scratched away. He knocked and heard thunderous barking coming from inside. When the door opened the dog bolted out into the yard and there in the doorway stood Keith! He was wearing a Roughrider t-shirt, open housecoat, grey military socks and he was holding a cup of coffee.

They both stood there, looking at one another for what seemed to be forever. Then Keith, in a disgusted voice said "Christ Tony, what the hell was that? My sister thinks I'm a drug dealer and my old man thinks there's a mob hit on me. Get in here; it's friggin cold out there."

Tony came in and looked around before sitting down at the small kitchen table. It wasn't much and there wasn't much but what was there was clean and tidy. Keith poured him a cup of coffee and sat down across from him.

"I owe you an explanation, I know that. I left you hanging and I know that too and I wouldn't blame you if you wanted to swing on me a few times, but I had no choice, Tony. I came back to town after my release to tell them I was heading to Winnipeg. I didn't get the chance. Ben and Susan had been fighting for some time and she had split to who knows where. Ben went on a drinking binge and hadn't sobered up and was staying with a friend of his. This was Ben's house, but it's mine now, as long as I can pay the rent. They both took off and left my little sister here to fend for herself. She's twelve Tony."

Keith was looking into his coffee cup. "The Welfare got wind of it and Child Services stepped in and was going to place her in a home. That's when I came on the scene and told them I would be her legal guardian and look after her. I don't have a job yet, but I'm looking. If you want to hit me, do it now, because Beth has to get off to school and I need to get a newspaper."

Keith's younger sister Beth came into the kitchen to grab her lunch before heading out. She had short blond hair, blue eyes and Tony could see she looked a lot like her older sister, but she was a lot more polite.

Tony introduced himself as her brother's best friend and out the door she went.

The guys talked most of the day and it was decided that Tony would stay a couple of days while he sorted things out as to his next move. It was clear to him that Keith wasn't going anywhere while his family needed him so Tony needed a plan.

They drove around town while Keith explained where things were and what made Saskatoon tick. Saskatoon was surrounded by farming and mining communities and a lot of the people from Saskatoon worked in these industries.

Tony looked around the city and liked it. It had lots of bridges and it felt good. After a long discussion with Keith and some soul searching, he decided to call Saskatoon home and settle down, which was something he'd never done. His release money from the military would be coming in soon and he needed to find a place to live and a job.

It really didn't take long for the guys to find work. Keith started working for the City. It seemed that Ben had a few friends there and pulled some strings. Tony answered an ad for an Operation Manager's position with a local security company and was accepted because of his military background.

Tony found a small house just around the corner from Keith and the guys hung out whenever they could. Things were coming together again. Keith had started dating a girl he met in the payroll office at his job and Tony dove into his new position, showing the bosses he could do the job. He was always on call and had little time to consider dating.

Chapter 25

Tony had been going out to the clubs but nothing had been turning up in terms of a hookup and he really wasn't looking for a relationship.

He had a few favourite places to drink and the ladies weren't half bad most of the time. He had heard that a Disco named Stoker's was a fun place and it was closing the next weekend. He'd never been there before so "what could it hurt?"

The next Friday night while drinking at his local bar with a friend, he remembered the Disco! His friend, Brian didn't need much coaxing. They jumped in Tony's car, and headed for the popular nightspot.

It was about half past midnight when they arrived and it was really packed. They walked around a bit, the music was loud and the lights were flashing. They grabbed a couple of drinks from the bar and continued to scan the room.

All the tables seemed to be occupied until they noticed a couple of empty seats at a table with three girls seated. They went over and introduced themselves and asked if they could join them.

The girls were funny and easy to talk to and Tony and Brian did have a good time.

It was about 5:00 AM when things started breaking up and the group said they're goodbyes. The girls mentioned that they would be there the following night, to close the place down and the guys should try and make it as well.

After sleeping in on Saturday Tony called Brian to see if he was going to show at Stoker's. Brian said that he got called to work and couldn't make it.

Tony decided he would catch some supper, have a couple of drinks and then head out to the disco, "what the hell!"

He walked through the door and was again greeted by loud music, blinding lights and wall to wall people. The place was jumping. The dance floor was full and the lineup to the bar stretched out to the patio.

Tony could see that he should have started going to the disco awhile ago, not just the last two nights.

He ordered a beer and walked the room, watching people dance all the while looking to see if the ladies from the night before were there. He also noticed other ladies laughing and having a good time. He decided that he was going to ask someone to dance but which one?

Tony moved to the left of the dance floor and out of the corner of his eye he noticed the group of three girls he had met the night before! They were laughing and pointing at the dance floor and moving to the music.

Chapter 26

Rebecca Fielding was born in Saskatoon, Saskatchewan to parents, Agnes and Peter who were born in small towns in Saskatchewan.

Once married, Agnes and Peter moved to Saskatoon where there was more work and they could raise their family.

Rebecca grew up, finished high school and attended Business College and eventually found a position in a large firm.

She had a small group of friends as well as her younger sister, Roberta who she hung around with. They were in their mid-twenties and single. Oh they had all had dates and flings but Rebecca had never had a real "relationship."

Rebecca was quickly becoming disillusioned. Oh, she had a good job and had been moving up the ladder over the previous eight years but something was definitely missing in her life.

She looked around the office and as she often did, noticed Flora. Flora was Rebecca's measuring stick for a successful life, not work, life. Flora was 40 something and single. She had been in her current position for almost 20 years! No doubt she was content but Rebecca looked at Flora with a feeling of dread. This is not what she wanted.

It was Friday again and for the last couple of years Rebecca and her friends had been going to a local after-hours disco called "Stoker's." They were tired of waiting around for some man to come along and they had decided that they may as well have some fun and who knew?

Rebecca and the other ladies had even decided that they weren't going to wait around like "wall flowers" and they would go ahead and do the asking. This was still pretty forward-thinking in 1979 and 1980 but they went ahead and asked and most often they actually had a good time.

They had a routine. Most Friday and Saturdays they would meet at Stoker's at 11:00 PM in the parking lot. Since it was an "after-hours" club, things didn't really get started until around midnight with most of the patrons coming in after the bars closed.

She looked over at Flora. Though her heart ached and it was Friday, she was fighting a migraine and decided she would not go to the club that night, even though she knew it was the last weekend that the club would be open. Disco music was winding down and music like Punk Rock and Grunge were becoming popular, so the club was closing.

With her head pounding and a cloud of doom hanging over her, Rebecca went home and fell asleep. She was awakened by her telephone at about 8:00 PM by one of her friends calling to find out if she was coming to the club. She sounded animated and excited! It was the last weekend they would have the club to go to. Rebecca didn't want to disappoint her friends but told her she was not feeling well and would not be going. Her friend told her that if she changed her mind everyone else would be there. With that they then said goodbye.

Rebecca had a hot shower and went to bed early, trying not to think about anything.

She slept late for her usual Saturday and around 11:00 AM her telephone started ringing off the hook. Her sister and two friends called, breathless as they told her what had transpired the previous night at the club.

They had indeed gone to the club and had a great time! Rebecca should have been there! They had met two guys who were funny, friendly, interesting and cute! The girls had invited them to come back Saturday night.

Furthermore, they told Rebecca that she really needed to come to the club on this last Saturday night. They told her that she would probably kick herself if she didn't make it. Besides, it would be their last time to be together as a group at the club.

Rebecca was beside herself. Her headache was ebbing, and she had had a good night sleep, so with some trepidation she made the decision to go.

Rebecca met her sister and two friends at the usual time, 11:00 PM. They found a table and all the girls were telling Rebecca again about the previous evening.

At around midnight patrons were arriving and the music was playing. Rebecca decided she should make a trip to the ladies room.

Chapter 27

Tony moved toward the table scrutinizing the ladies he had met the night before. They were young, around 25 or so, "maybe one of them would like to dance with this handsome devil," he thought.

As he approached the table recognition beamed on the ladies' faces. "You made it!" said Roberta. The other two ladies were equally excited. Tony approached and told them he was glad he found the place but his friend was not able to come. They began trying to have a conversation over the din of the music.

Before leaving the ladies' room Rebecca checked her reflection in the mirror and headed back to her table. As she drew nearer she noted the newcomer sitting with her friends. She approached the table and was immediately introduced to one of the gentlemen that Rebecca's friends had met the night before. Roberta piped up "Rebecca, this is Tony!"

Tony had been sitting with his back to Rebecca. He turned around at the introduction, and looked at the young woman who had approached and forgot why he had come over to the table, she was beautiful! She had brown, short curly hair, brown eyes that drew him in. She wore glasses and had a perfect smile.

She was wearing a black skirt that Tony thought fit her well and a white sleeveless top with a small collar that had some type of design on it and completed her. To Tony she was stunning and everyone else in the room faded away. She extended her hand and as it slid into Tony's she said "my name is Rebecca, and you are?"

Tony sat there holding her hand for a second or two and then finally remembered his name "Tony, my name is Tony."

She was stunning and Tony was a mess.

Chapter 28

Rebecca's dark mood was still hovering and thought Tony had probably returned because he was interested in one of the other girls.

He was pleasant, Rebecca noted, she agreed he was cute and funny. He talked animatedly and actually performed a few table tricks.

At some point shortly thereafter, Rebecca relaxed and started examining him more carefully. She noticed that he didn't seem particularly interested in any of her companions and found herself wishing he would ask her to dance.

Rebecca's wish was granted shortly thereafter. After talking to him for awhile Tony asked her if she wanted to dance. Rebecca nodded and Tony took her hand and led her to the dance floor. They only left the dance floor once and that was for refreshments.

It seemed to Tony that they were having a great time and they danced until closing at 5:00 AM. They all walked to the parking lot and over to their cars. Tony walked Rebecca over to hers. He told her that he was happy they met and they should get together for coffee or dinner if she wanted. Rebecca smiled at Tony and gave him her telephone number and told him to call if he wanted. With that he kissed her, and then she was gone.

It was dawn, and Tony was exhausted but he could not get Rebecca out of his head. He checked his pockets to be sure that he indeed had her phone number. Sleep, he needed sleep.

Chapter 29

Tony woke late in the afternoon and checked his pocket again. Yes, it was there.

He tried to get a few things done around the house that day but his mind kept going to the previous night and Rebecca. Finally around 6:00 PM he phoned, but wasn't sure what he was going to say. To his dismay there was no answer.

He tried again at 9:00 PM, this time with success! Rebecca answered and all Tony could think of to say was "Is the coffee on?"

Chapter 30

Rebecca went home and tried to sleep, wondering when and if she would see him again.

As was her habit, she went to her mother's house for dinner on Sunday. She and Roberta told their mother about their last night at the club.

Rebecca returned home at about 8:00 PM and began readying herself for work the next day. Her thoughts returned to Tony.

At around 9:00 PM her telephone rang and she answered quickly, her stomach doing a flip and her heart skipping a beat, it was him!

There was a hesitation and then he asked "is the coffee on?

"It can be, she answered, are you coming over?" Tony replied "is it too soon?"

"I think I can give you a coffee," she said. She gave him her address and twenty minutes later he was at her door! Tony was surprised how close it was to his place. They kissed and she led him to the couch where she nervously served him coffee.

Tony came into a modestly furnished apartment that was tidy and clean. The biggest thing in the room was a piano. "Do you play?" he asked.

"Trying to, it's a work in progress," Rebecca answered.

They talked until midnight. They spoke about Rebecca's job, her family and Saskatoon in general. Tony told her about his time in the military, where he was from and the fact that he was in Saskatoon because of his long time friend.

They spoke about everything it seemed, including his apparent hatred for peas!

Tony was 27 years old and Rebecca was 26. He asked to see her driver's license because he thought she was younger. Rebecca laughed but showed him.

The conversation was easy and Rebecca hated to say goodnight but it was around midnight and Tony asked if she wanted to get together during the week.

"Call me," she said.

They kissed again, this time a little longer and they promised to connect in a few days. Then Tony was out the door.

Chapter 31

Tony's rental was small and very old, but it was really all he could afford, so he made the best of it. You had to go outside to change your mind and you could just about touch both walls with your arms opened. He liked it, for now.

It had been a day since he had seen Rebecca but she was never far from his thoughts. "Should he invite her over? Was it too early to be so bold? Would she say no? That would be bad" Tony thought. He waited most of the next day and then dialed her number.

The phone rang and rang and rang, then "hello."

"Hi Rebecca, it's me Tony. Am I disturbing you?"

"Not at all," she said. "I was beginning to think you wouldn't call."

"Damn, I'm sorry about that," Tony replied. "I didn't want to seem pushy." Then there was a long awkward silence.

Finally, Rebecca said "so, what's up?"

"What are you doing right now?" Tony probed.

"Not too much," she answered.

Tony continued "hey, do you think you might want to come over for coffee? I owe you coffee and you can see my place, it's just down the street."

There was more silence and then relief. "You bet," she replied, "just let me freshen up and I'll be right over!"

Tony gave her his address and said goodbye. As he hung up the phone, panic set in. He knew he liked Rebecca and wanted to make a good impression. The place wasn't too tidy because most of the time he just wasn't there. Keith's place was just six houses down and around the corner so he was there most nights.

He started running around the house straightening things up and hiding his laundry. He tried to imagine what he would say when she got there, when an alarm bell went off in his head. He looked and confirmed his worst nightmare. He had no coffee!

A light knock on the door brought him to reality and he moved to the door to open it. She was standing in the doorway, waiting for him to welcome her in. Tony just stood there, searching for the right thing to say. He fell apart when the only thing that came out of his mouth was "I cleaned for you!" His mind slipped back into gear and a loud voice in his head yelled "what the hell man, did you really say that?"

"That's nice," she replied.

Tony still wasn't moving. "Can I come in?" she asked.

"Please, please," he replied, "you're my first visitor."

Rebecca stepped through the door. Tony was again lost for words as she passed by him and he caught the scent of her perfume. "Like I said on the phone," he fumbled, "the place is small and manageable."

She looked around at the small living room and was surprised to see how clean it was. Moving to the kitchen, which was the biggest room in the house, she saw a small table, fridge and stove.

Tony broke her train of thought. "I don't eat here much, so things generally stay where they are. I don't have a lot of plates and stuff and only two cups which brings me to my next confession. I don't have any coffee either, but I do have Tang."

She smiled and shook her head. "No one drinks Tang, do they?" She passed by him on her way to the next room and her perfume melted him where he stood. "What's this room?" she asked.

"That's the bedroom," Tony replied as he moved to block her way. "Please don't look. I said I cleaned, but that doesn't mean everything."

"How bad can it be?" she said as she brushed by him in the doorway.

Tony was aware of her body heat as she passed by and moved closer to take her in his arms. They kissed passionately and for what seemed like an eternity before they pulled away to breathe and look into each other's eyes.

He kissed her again and whispered in her ear "I want you Rebecca."

"Oh yes, Tony," she replied softly.

What seemed like forever, but not near long enough they finally fell asleep and they awoke hours later wanting the coffee that wasn't there. They tried to shower only to awaken their desires again and were driven from the shower when the hot water ran out.

They dressed quickly and laughed at what had just happened. "Come on," said Tony, "I promised you coffee." Out the door and five minutes later they were at a coffee shop, sitting across from each other sipping hot coffee and smelling the fresh baked goods that were all around them though neither of them was hungry.

They started to speak at the same time, stopped and laughed at their awkwardness. "When can I see you again Rebecca?" he asked.

A small frown came over her face before she answered. "I have to go out of town for a few days. My best friend is getting married, but I will call you when I get back." Tony wasn't sure if he could wait that long, but he managed to say goodbye and they parted ways again.

After Rebecca left, Tony busied himself with his work and got together with Keith a lot. He was coming to the realization that working for a security company was not all that it was cracked up to be. Mostly it was babysitting low-paid guards and making sure they showed up where they were supposed to. Most of them only stayed for a paycheck or two and then Tony would have to look for replacements. He didn't see a future in this, but for now it would have to do. Now there was Rebecca.

Chapter 32

Rebecca hated to leave but Tony assured her they'd see each other again soon. She was going to her girlfriend's wedding on Friday and Saturday but would be back Sunday. Tony asked her to call him as soon as she was back.

Friday arrived and Rebecca left for her girlfriend's wedding in a small town 50 miles outside of Saskatoon. While she drove her mind went back to the little house on Edwards Avenue.

Rebecca and the bride had been friends for years and she told her she had "met someone!" She was given the bride's blessing to leave early Sunday morning.

She arrived back home at 11:00 AM and immediately called Tony. He answered on the first ring. Without much thought Rebecca asked him if he would like to come over for dinner. They agreed on the time of 6:30 PM and said they were excited to see each other again.

Though excited, Rebecca busied herself with tidying and buying groceries for their dinner.

As she walked down the aisles of the store, she wondered what Tony might like. She remembered her mother once telling her that the way to a man's heart is through his stomach. She knew that this was just one of those "old wives tales."

She decided on stew, wholesome and comforting.

She brought her groceries home and started cooking. She babied the meat and then went to add vegetables: potatoes, celery, carrots and she had a package of frozen vegetables containing beans, corn and CRAP! Peas!

So with the determination of a woman smitten, she painstakingly removed all the peas. Problem solved!

She cheated a little and bought a sponge cake, turning it into strawberry shortcake.

At precisely 6:30 PM Tony knocked on the door. Rebecca opened it and there he was holding a bottle of sparkling wine.

They kissed like lovers who hadn't seen each other for weeks! She then invited him to sit while she finished putting dinner together. Tony poured the wine.

Though dinner was good, neither tasted it. They were chatting and Tony looked down at his plate and thought "that's odd." He asked her about the vegetables, noting that every vegetable was in the stew, except for peas.

Rebecca blushed and told him what had happened with the peas because she remembered that he didn't like them.

Tony's stomach did a flip and he reached for her hand, squeezed it and said gently; "it's canned peas I don't like."

They both stared into each other's eyes and laughed.

Before dessert Rebecca started cleaning off the table and Tony helped. It was a comfortable exercise and they chatted while they busied themselves.

When Rebecca finished at the sink, she turned and found Tony standing directly behind her. He gently told her he couldn't get over the "peas" thing. No one had ever done anything for him like that before. She dropped her gaze and Tony lifted her chin and kissed her. Dessert was forgotten. They went to bed, but not to sleep.

Chapter 33

Tony and Rebecca were seeing each other every minute they could and when they weren't together, they were on the phone. They never seemed to run out of things to talk about.

Tony spent more and more time at Rebecca's and eventually moved in. They were inseparable. At the end of the summer he met her family. He liked them all but the one he took a shine to most, was Rebecca's mom. She was a small, frail woman with a sense of humour, a strength-of-character and determination. She had lost her husband a few years prior to Tony coming into the picture and at times he could see a loneliness that lurked just beneath the surface. He liked to tease her and she gave him back as good as she got.

Before Christmas while Tony was talking to his boss, the conversation turned to possibilities for promotion. He was happy with Tony's work and a position would be coming open in the spring, in Regina and he asked Tony if he thought he would be interested. Tony's head was reeling. The conversation ended with his boss telling him to think about it.

He thought back to Goose Bay and Gloria. At that time when Tony received a transfer, Gloria wanted desperately to go with him, but he realized that that wasn't something he wanted.

This time was different, just thinking of leaving Saskatoon and saying goodbye to Rebecca made Tony a little crazy. For the first time he couldn't imagine his life without her. He wanted to grow and he was done with the job in Saskatoon, but what was he going to do? He would wait through the holidays before he thought about it again.

It didn't take that long. Two days before Christmas, while searching the malls for just the right gift for her, he found himself in front of a jewelry store. "Earrings," he thought and went in.

The store was busy with other people searching for just the right gift. The store clerk told him it would be a few minutes and Tony decided to look around. He wound up in front of a jewelry case full of rings, engagement rings! Timing is everything. The store clerk came over and asked him if she could show him something.

About an hour later Tony walked out with a heightened sense of excitement; he had bought a ring!!! He wasn't even sure how he had gotten the nerve, wasn't sure what Rebecca would say, but he knew he didn't want to go to Regina without her!

It was really hard for Tony to keep his secret quiet; he was excited but also scared, "what if she said no?"

On Christmas Eve he bought a bottle of wine and waited for Rebecca to get home from work.

He made a light supper and even put candles on the table. When Rebecca came through the door at 5:30 he nearly jumped out of his skin. This was it, show time!

Rebecca was pleased, Tony had never gotten supper together for her before, and the wine was excellent. After the longest dinner he had ever had Tony started telling Rebecca about the discussion he had had with his boss and the possibility of a promotion and transfer.

Rebecca looked a little shocked. She said she was excited for him. Deep down she was worried that this life she and Tony had been living might soon be over before it even got started.

Before Rebecca could voice her thoughts to Tony, he got up from his chair and left the room. A minute later he came back, knelt down in front of her and held out a little box to her.

Rebecca was completely taken by surprise! She took the little box while her heart did flips. She opened it and found the sweetest engagement ring! At the same time Tony said in a voice that cracked full of emotion. "Will you come with me Rebecca and marry me?"

The tears started flowing and she put her arms around Tony and gave him a swift "yes!"

Rebecca and Tony didn't wait long; they married at the court house in Saskatoon on a clear, bright, cold winter day.

Chapter 34

Soon after they were married, Tony received a promotion to General Manager for the Security Company, and with that, the transfer to Regina. This was not something Rebecca had imagined since she had never been away from home. Tony was her home now and her fear of staying at one job for the rest of her life and becoming like "Flora" had ended. This would be the next step in her continuing adventures with Tony.

There was another first for Tony and Rebecca; they were able to buy a small house. They were thrilled!

Tony's new job in Regina was not new at all. He was still constantly looking for guards, only now he also had to find them work in the form of new contracts.

He kept in contact with Keith and managed to get together with him whenever he was in the Saskatoon office. Tony sat back at his desk looking at his schedule for the day, when the phone rang and he picked it up. Like always, thinking nothing of it. This call was anything but normal. It was Keith.

"Tony, are you sitting down? I've got some bad news for you, man." Tony's senses came alive. "I just got a call from Ron in North Bay. Rick Bagley is dead!"

Tony was shocked and frozen to his chair. Rick was one of Tony's best friends. They had gone through boot camp together along with five other guys that had each others' backs and had called themselves the "rat pack."

His voice rose "what do you mean dead? How? When? Are you sure?"

Keith told Tony what Ron Van Meter had said. "Rick had been found in a back alley about a week ago in downtown Montreal, beaten, stabbed and left for dead. He had been found by a drunk that came out of a building to take a piss and reported the body to the police. Rick had been identified by his military ID card and driver's license that had been strewn around his body. There was no wallet. The police contacted the Base Commander to pass on the news. Bad news like this travels fast in the military. Before long, Ron got word of it and phoned Keith and the rest of the pack. The police had no clues and were calling it a mugging gone badly. "Just another statistic" they said.

"That's bullshit," Tony caught himself yelling in the phone. "Where is he now?"

Keith told Tony that Rick's body had been released to his parents and they were having him transported back to Bosen in Northern Ontario that week. Hundreds of memories of his friends all came back to him at once.

"When's the burial?" Tony asked.

"The burial is Friday Tony," Keith replied sadly.

"Get your shit together," Tony howled. "We're going to be there. Get some time off or something, but be ready to leave today!"

"How are we going to do this Tony?" Keith asked.

"If we drive all night and tomorrow we can be there in 25 hours or so. I'm coming for you Keith, be ready." With that, Tony hung up the phone.

He told the Office Manager that there was a family emergency and he wouldn't be back for some time as he hurried out the door to tell Rebecca what had happened.

Tony told her that he loved her but had to go to his friend. He told her he would stay in touch and get back to her as soon as he could.

Rebecca knew that Tony's bond with his military brothers was strong and she could see that he was hurting inside. She packed a bag for him as he made a few calls, trying to get more information and within 30 minutes he was out the door heading for Saskatoon.

Chapter 35

Keith was waiting for him when he drove up and jumped in the front seat without saying a word. Tony looked over at him and said "are we good man?" Keith didn't answer, just nodded his head.

The entire trip east was a mass of unanswered questions and speculation as to why Rick was in the alley, but one thing was for sure, they were going to find out.

Trees, trees and more trees, that's all Ontario was about, that and the lakes. The guys drove through Toronto and turned north up to cottage country and beyond, finally seeing the log mills and drove passed them to the sleepy town of Bosen. They didn't see it right away because of the massive trees, but as they turned left to crest a hill; there it was.

There was a main street that was no more than two blocks long, with a four way stop in the middle. There were a few small shops, a hardware store, a post office, a bar

called "Timbers," a Loblaws and a corner café called
Livey's.

The whole town was cut into the surrounding forest and
in the distance, the log mill itself. It was massive, dark and
never ending smoke billowed out of its four mighty stacks.
Everything was covered in what looked like dust and the
strong smell of the mill and lumber being processed was
everywhere. You could feel the heaviness of the dust when
you breathed the air.

The guys stopped at the tiny post office to ask the teller
for the address to the Bagley's home. This was met with
cutting eyes from the teller, and many questions about why
they were here and why they were asking. As far as the teller
was concerned, the guys were strangers and not to be
trusted.

It took them several minutes to convince the suspicious
old woman that they were there to pay their respects to the
Bagley family and say goodbye to their friend.

She had tears in her eyes as she gave Tony directions to
the Bagley home. "The whole town is in shock," she said,
near crying as she wiped a tear from her reddening eyes.
"Poor Janet, she's destroyed. That boy was her whole life. It
broke her heart when he joined the military and moved

away, but she talked about him every day to anyone who would listen."

The boys turned to leave and missed seeing the old woman sit back in her chair and wipe tears from her eyes. "It just isn't fair," she mumbled to herself as they left the building.

They moved out onto the street and were again assaulted by the smell of the old mill and the old town. "No wonder Rick wanted to leave this place," Keith said quietly to his friend.

They got back into the car and drove down the street to the four way stop, turning left. The townspeople were out and about and watched them roll slowly by. Down another hundred yards, left again and up a small driveway they came upon an old trailer that had deteriorated many years ago. It used to be white and green, Tony guessed, but the colors faded away long ago to become a grey something color with green trim and a rusting skirting.

The porch was just old grey wood with a plank missing and was held together with a few nails and cinderblock stairs. There was an old rusted Ford truck in the driveway that looked like it hadn't moved in awhile and tied to it was a nasty dog that hated strangers and would have ripped Tony and Keith apart if it ever got a chance.

They didn't have to knock; the dog had alerted the occupants to their arrival. The boys stepped onto the porch. The door burst open and a short grey-haired old man pointed a shotgun at them in defiance. He was in his 60's, thin with a week's worth of beard on his leathered face.

Even though the man was hunched over, Tony could tell that he had worked hard all his life and trusted no one. "State your business and get the hell off my property!" he growled.

Tony took a deep breath and looked at the old man straight on. "My name is Tony Simons and this is Keith Stoddard. We were Rick's best friends in the military and we have driven here from Saskatchewan to pay our last respects to one of our own."

From behind the angry old man a small thin arm came around and a hand touched the gun. "It's okay Ron, put the gun down." A small frail voice could be heard from behind him. "I know these young men, Rickie told me about them in his letters and on the phone." The old man moved aside to reveal a tiny old woman with aged skin, crippled hands and grey hair that was pulled back in a bun. She moved in front of her protector and extended her hand to the boys. "I'm Janet Bagley and this is Ron. You're here to see Rick?" she asked quietly. Tony nodded his head. "He'll be happy to see you," she said. "You're here for the service on Friday, I hope?"

Tony told her "yes, we are."

She led them down the narrow hall of the trailer to a small back bedroom. "This is Rick's room," she said as she patted the door. "He really liked being in here when he was home. I haven't touched anything. He didn't like people touching his stuff."

She opened the door to the small bedroom, let them in and closed the door behind her as she left.

The little room was spotless and turned out like a military sleeping area in the barracks, complete with hospital corner made bed and a military locker with all his clothes folded and pressed. The walls were full of Rick's military pictures, course photos and a Station Commander's Commendation for something he had done some time back.

The room was perfect except for one thing, the urn that sat in the middle of the perfectly made bed that held their friend's last remains.

Grief welled up in Tony's throat and he swallowed hard as he continued to stare at the object in the middle of the bed. "Christ," Keith said in a low voice and then went silent.

They stayed in the room for about 10 minutes or so, then left and quietly closed the door. Janet was waiting for them on the other side and walked them back to the living area. "Please sit down," she said, "I'll make you some tea."

They talked about Rick for a few hours, the military and the guys he trained with. There were funny stories shared by all, and Janet was becoming more relaxed.

Tony chose his questions carefully, but wanted to know what the police had told her and what they were doing to find Rick's killer.

She knew little of what happened, only that Rick had phoned her two nights before the tragedy and said he'd be coming home in a couple of days with something to tell her and Ron. First he had to be someplace or meet someone the next night. He told her he loved her and that was the last time she spoke to him.

"The police are calling it 'unfortunate' and a 'robbery gone badly." Tony could see that Janet was getting upset again so the boys got up to leave, promising her to be at the funeral on Friday.

As they went out the door Tony could hear Janet saying to Ron "Rick's home now, this is where he's going to stay."

They got in the car and looked at each other in disbelief. Keith sighed and in a very low voice said "Holy shit Tony, I thought I was going to die."

Chapter 36

They stayed in the only hotel in town that probably had a rating just shy of a dive hostel and ate at the only diner in town on the corner.

Friday morning came quickly and the boys found themselves on the other side of town at a small church that was filled with the town's folk and a minister. The guys were sitting at the back of the church trying not to be noticed, but it didn't work because as the service started the doors opened up and in walked two men in full military uniforms with their hats in their hands.

Tony recognized them immediately; it was Ron Van Meter and Steve Langsford. They moved in and sat next to Tony and Keith and were quiet for the whole service. They helped lower Rick's urn into its final resting place and said goodbye. Then they moved to the roadside to shake each other's hands and say how good it was to see each other even at such a sad time.

Ron and Steve were there just for the day and would have to leave in the morning, so there was much to talk about and little time to do it.

They all said goodbye to Mrs. Bagley and were about to drive away when she moved to Tony's car window and handed him a folder. "This is the police report," she said. "Maybe you can make something out of it, I can't." She thanked them again, turned and was gone.

The four friends drove to the diner on the corner and took a booth, away from prying eyes. "How did you two get here?" Tony asked.

Van spoke up first. "We knew we were coming but had to set up flights and passes. You know we have to leave tomorrow, but we're here now. We couldn't let Rick pass by himself."

"Didn't know you two were coming," Steve said. "Since you two got out, you're kind of hard to follow. Why did you get out, Tony?"

"Long story," Tony said. "I'll tell you one of these days and just so you know, I do miss it."

The guys had dinner and talked the night away until it was time to say goodbye. They shook hands and promised to stay in touch and with that Ron and Steve drove away.

There was nothing left for Tony and Keith to do but pack up and head back. Tony was sitting on the cot, waiting for Keith. He reached down and picked up the folder Rick's mom had given him.

Most of it was reports and pictures of Rick and the place he was found. They had taken pictures of his military ID, his driver's license along with things that were near his body and under it. There were business cards and a key from a hotel where he had been staying.

The key was from the hotel "Capital Hill." Tony's mind was racing. "What was Rick doing there?" he asked out loud as Keith came into the room.

"What was who doing where?" Keith asked.

"I'll explain on the way. We're going to Montreal!"

Chapter 37

Two hours later Tony was still explaining his theory to Keith; that Rick was there for a reason nobody knew about and then he was going home to talk to his parents. "Why?" Tony said out loud. "We are going to have to look at where Rick was found and the hotel he was staying in."

The address was on the picture of the hotel key and after many hours of searching, because they couldn't speak or read French, they located the Capital Hotel in a less than desirable part of the city, called "The Stroll."

The Capital Hotel was just this side of a flop house and the marquee sign above the old door flickered and crackled in the light rain. It was dimly lit inside, old and dusty and smelled like something that was not healthy.

The lady behind the check-in counter looked old and hard and had too much makeup on and was smoking a cigarillo. She eyed them carefully as Tony approached the desk. "Qu'est-ce que vous voulez?" She hissed.

"Do you speak English?" Keith said from a distance.

"When I have to," she grinned; "when it's good for business. Are you lost little English boys?" she said moving forward. "Can Lizzy help you?"

She put her arm around Tony's waist and moved closer. Tony came back to his senses just in time to avoid having his ass grabbed. "Our friend stayed here a couple of weeks ago," he blurted.

Lizzy was slowly trying to remove Tony's wallet as he moved away. "What friend?" she said slowly. "What is his name English boy?"

Tony looked right at her "Rick Bagley was his name." He watched for her reaction. Her eyebrow raised a little and Tony knew he hit a nerve.

"You mean the young man that was murdered across the street in the alley?" she stared back. "Yes, he stayed here a lot," she offered. "Two, three days here, two three days there; he was a regular. He was sometimes alone, sometimes not, but when he was not, he was always with the same pretty little French girl with flaming red hair. The police have been here many times," Lizzy smiled. "They have asked many questions and searched the room many times. I told them nothing. They didn't pay. Murder is bad for business," she whispered.

She moved back to the counter and grabbed another smoke.

"We want to see his room," Keith spoke up.

Lizzy smiled again, "you can see it, of course, in about half an hour; it's occupied. Have a seat," she said, "relax. Do you want a drink or something a little stronger?"

Tony and Keith reluctantly sat down on a couch that looked as bad as it smelled. He could feel his ass tighten up as he sunk into the fabric.

True to her word a half hour passed and a short, fat, bald little man came down the squeaky stairs and handed Lizzy a key and some money.

"Give it a minute, gentlemen, the maid has to clean up," she chuckled. Down the stairs came the nastiest old hooker Tony had ever seen with a rolled up sheet under her arm. Throwing it in a basket, she disappeared around the corner.

"Your room is ready, gentlemen," she smiled sweetly. "Please, enjoy your stay at the Capital, that'll be $20 English, in advance, 2nd floor, room 202."

The room was exactly as promised, a room. It was dimly lit and smelled like sweaty bodies. The floor was damp and sticky, a night stand and a wooden chair completed the décor and the view was stunning. It looked right down on the alleyway where Rick was murdered.

Tony looked out the window for a long time. There were buildings, lots of old buildings and the odd flashing neon sign. "What was his friend doing here," he thought. "Was it sex or drugs? Even Rick wouldn't come here for that. There had to be another reason." Tony's mind was moving a mile a minute.

Keith was looking around in disbelief. "He wouldn't come here unless he had to, Tony." Keith sighed and asked "what was it that drove Rick to this hotel, and this room?"

Tony was rubbing his eyes. It had been a very long day. He was sitting on the chair, looking at the file again and Keith was looking out the window. The street he saw was old and badly lit. The cars came and went, dropping people off and picking them up near a building across the street with a small blue neon sign of what looked to Keith like a bird in a cage.

Tony came to the window and watched the activity. "I haven't a clue what that is, man," he sighed. He moved back to the chair. He was tired and wanted to call it a night. He picked up the police file and was about to tell Keith they should leave when at the back of his clouded mind a picture formed, "bird in a cage." He had seen that picture before, but where? Suddenly he remembered and opened Rick's file one more time. There among the many papers and pictures, was what he was looking for, the photo of a business card with no writing on it, just the image of a bird in a cage.

Tony's eyes widened as he rose and showed Keith the card. Keith looked at the card and said "Holy shit, Tony, what is it?"

"I don't know, but I know who can tell us."

Down the stairs they went and right up to the counter again. Lizzy slowly got up from her chair and moved toward them. "That was fast," she smiled. "Should I send up housekeeping?" she giggled.

Tony didn't jump at the bait. He opened the file on the counter and removed the picture of the business card. "Can you tell me what this is?" he asked.

Lizzy looked down at the picture and back to Tony. "Looks like $20 to me English boy," she grinned. Tony shook his head and put the money on the counter, but didn't let it go.

Lizzy looked at the picture again and put her hand on the twenty. "La cage a oiseaux" she said.

Tony wasn't buying it this time. "In English," he said and was pulling the money away.

"The Bird Cage," she snapped. "It's across the street."

Tony released the bill. "What is it?" he asked.

"Club de striptease." Before Tony could ask again Lizzy finished the conversation by walking away; "a strip club, English boy."

It was like Tony had been hit with a baseball bat. "What the hell was Rick doing with a card from a nasty strip club in old Montreal?"

Keith looked at his friend and shook his head. "We're going over there, aren't we?"

Tony nodded and was heading for the door but didn't get out before hearing Lizzy one more time.

"Remember what I said, English boy, don't get dead, it's bad for business!"

Out into the night they went. It was still drizzling and made everything cold and damp. People were moving around with their heads down or covered because of the weather.

They crossed the street with every intention of entering the club but they were met by a huge dark-skinned man blocking their path. They hadn't even seen him until he was right in their faces.

"Ce que vous voulez ici?" he growled at them.

Tony spoke first because Keith was frozen in his tracks. "Do you speak English?"

The dark man spat back "what do you want English, you do not belong here."

"Just looking to see a show and have a beer," Tony replied. "Lizzy, across the street told us this was the place to be."

The man looked long at them and finally nodded his head.

As he opened the door, he spoke in a low tone over Tony's shoulder "have a beer, watch the show, don't make trouble, or I will come find you and you will pay."

Tony and Keith stepped by the bouncer and entered into a horror show. They hadn't seen anything like this before. The smoke was so thick you could cut it with a knife. It was dark as dark could be with only low lighting over what was known to be a bar.

The man behind the bar was short, bald and wore glasses down around the end of his nose. He was smoking what looked like a big nasty cigar and kept spitting pieces of it out on the floor. His once clean wife-beater t-shirt was long past white, now it was grey to black with stains of sweat. He had a bar towel slung over his rounded shoulder that he was constantly wiping his forehead and damp hands on.

Men dressed in all manner of dark clothing were crowded around the bar drinking and laughing at something they were talking about. There were many tables in the room and chairs around a small stage that consisted of a pole and one light trained on the centre of it.

The room smelled of beer, urine, smoke and marijuana.

The boys took seats as far away from the stage as they could with their backs to the wall. They prayed no one there would strike up a conversation. They ordered a beer and continued to watch everything.

Tony had so many questions swimming around in his head, one of which was why Rick had come to this hell hole. He looked at Keith and said in a low voice "what was he thinking? Where was his head?" Keith looked at him but didn't answer.

The music started up and out of the darkness, the past jumped out at them into the light. They were back in St. Savar, in "The Den" some six years before in a strip club with a mother/daughter team of dancers that drove the young military men crazy with every move.

She looked much older now, tired and drained. The life she chose had not been kind to her. She was slower, heavier and had harsh makeup on that wasn't hiding the age lines like it used to. She didn't smile; she just went through her routine, staring into space, trying to get the old men to give her money or drinks. They weren't buying it and at the end of her dance she hadn't even broke a sweat. She just walked off the stage to the appreciation of one or two old drunks in the corner that couldn't see her anyway.

Tony was floored. Keith was staring and said "Holy Shit; it's Lucy."

"What is she doing in this toilet of a bar," Tony gasped. "Why was Rick here watching this dried up, tired old woman trying to dance after all these years?"

The questions kept filling Tony's head until the answer he was looking for stepped out of the darkness into the light.

All the men in the bar crowded around the stage, clapping their hands and whistling loudly. This is who they came to see.

She was stunning, around 5'6 or taller in her high heels, no more than 120 pounds, deep blue eyes, and flaming red hair that moved on its own to the rhythm of the music.

She drove the men in the bar crazy and drained them of their money before the routine was over. The little pout she gave them before disappearing into the darkness brought the house down.

It was clearer now to Tony. Rick had somehow crossed paths with Lucy and became involved with her daughter, Elise. How long had it been going on? Only she knew now.

Tony had to talk to her. They waited outside in their car across the street for the club to finally close. It was 3:00 AM. They caught some movement down the street and saw her getting into a car. Somehow she had gotten by them, but that didn't matter. What did matter was talking to her tonight.

"Don't lose her Tony," Keith urged. Montreal does not sleep and apparently, neither did Elise. Half an hour later she pulled into a coffee shop and took a booth near the door. The café was well lit and her long red hair was in contrast with the white walls. Even from the parking lot, Tony and Keith could tell it was her. She was striking.

"We have to talk to her," Keith said, "and now." Tony nodded his head and they stepped out of the car, slowly walking across the parking lot and into the café. There were no formalities. The guys moved right to her booth and sat down across from her.

At first she was shocked at their boldness and began reaching for something in her purse. "Who the hell are you?" she snapped. "One more move and I will stab you both in the heart and leave you to die."

They heard the knife snap open.

Tony sat back and confronted her head on. "Like you did to our friend Rick in the alleyway next to the club a couple of weeks ago? Did you get that ape at the front door of the club to beat him senseless before you plunged that knife into him, you bitch." Tony was shaking with rage and Keith had to put his hand on his shoulder to calm him down.

Tony was not ready for what happened next. It was like he had slapped her across the face and she went into shock and burst into tears. There was no consoling her now. It was like a damn bursting, tears and babbling all at once.

"We were in love!" Elise cried into her hands. "We were going to be together! He asked me to marry him. I was the happiest girl in the world. We went to tell my mom and she broke into a rage. Elise could tell she remembered Rick immediately. She had told Elise many times about how he had gotten her panties in a club years before and was surprised that he had found her and her daughter after all this time. She hated the fact that this Englishman was in love with her little Elise and threatened him if he continued the affair.

That was months ago in another city but we got together again in secret when Lucy moved her show to Montreal. Rick stayed across the street from the Bird Cage and I came to him whenever I could. That dark night of the murder, Rick told me that he was going to see Lucy and tell her he was taking me away. I begged him not to. That was the last time I saw him alive.

"The police said it was a mugging. This was not so. Lucy confronted me in the dressing room later that night and told me that he would not be bothering us anymore and it was back to the way it was supposed to be, just the two of them, always. She had killed him that night," Elise said, "I know it. I wanted to tell someone but I was so scared."

Tony was stunned with what he was hearing, he couldn't move. He just sat there and stared at her. Keith spoke first as he reached over to hold her hand, "you have to go to the police, Elise, and we will take you there. You'll be safe, we promise."

She wiped her eyes and took a deep breath, "I know," she said, "it's time."

They left the café and drove to the Police Station, spoke to the detectives and gave their statements. Elise was placed in protective custody and the next morning Lucy and her bodyguard were arrested for Rick's murder.

Tony and Keith sat in the same café where they had confronted Elise two nights before, little was being said. Coffee was being quietly sipped. Finally, Keith looked up at his friend and said "let's go home, buddy, we're done here."

They rose from the booth, paid their tab and walked over to their car. "You drive, Keith," Tony sighed, "I'm tired."

Chapter 38

The trip back was uneventful and the guys took turns catching up on their sleep and talking like magpies. A cloud had been lifted and it was good, knowing that Rick could rest now and Tony and Keith could get on with their lives.

They gabbed about how good it was to see the other guys again, all decked out in their uniforms, if only for a brief time. They would be happy he knew, when they were told that Rick's murder was solved and Tony and Keith had a hand in it.

They talked about Saskatoon and Regina and where their lives ended up. Tony told his friend that working for a security company had no future in it and that he'd be applying at the Regina Police Department as soon as he got back. He was hoping his military background would count for something.

Keith smiled at him and laughed. "I always knew you'd be back in some kind of uniform," he chuckled.

Tony dropped his friend off in "Toon town" and he was home in another two hours, sitting on the couch with Rebecca, telling her everything that had happened. She was shocked, happy and sad all at once and hugged him tightly. "I'm glad you're ok Tony, I missed you terribly." With that, they fell into each other's arms.

The next day Tony went back to work. It was like he had never left, unhappy customers, missing guards and complaining office workers.

When he got home that night, he sat Rebecca down at the kitchen table and told her how much he missed the military but if he hadn't released, he would never have met her, so getting out was a blessing. He would always be there for her but he had to make a change in careers and fast. He told her that he was thinking of applying with the Regina Police Department and asked her what her thoughts on this move would be.

Rebecca knew Tony missed the military and the structure of the job and she knew he wouldn't put himself in harm's way without thinking about it first. She loved him and gave him her blessing.

The next day Tony filled out his application with the police department and was told that it would be reviewed and they would get back to him shortly. Now it was a waiting game.

A week went by, then two and Tony was beginning to doubt himself and wondered if his application was strong enough. Then Friday afternoon as Tony sat at his desk, waiting for the miserable week to end. The radio was on and some pretty good music was playing so he let his mind wander.

There were commercials, music, more commercials and then his ears perked up and could not believe what he was hearing. The Canadian Military found that their organization was short of skilled tradesmen in certain fields and were looking for ex members to re-enlist with no penalties and return of rank.

Tony sat up in his chair. That was the coolest thing he'd ever heard. Then the announcer went on to read the list of trades required. There in the middle of the whole thing was "AD Tech 171." "Holy shit!" he said out loud to himself.

Half an hour later a call came in from Saskatoon. It was Keith. "Did you hear what's happening?" he asked. "Do you believe it?"

"That's wild, buddy," Tony replied. "I knew they released too many tradesmen, now they need us back."

"What are you going to do now, Tony buddy?" Keith was fishing.

"I'm going to talk to Rebecca and think about it over the weekend. "How about you Pilgrim? You got the itch?" now Tony was fishing.

"I've got to talk to my sister and see how she feels about this. Let's talk again Monday." With that, the conversation ended.

Tony closed the office and drove home with his head swimming with possibilities for the future and couldn't wait to talk to Rebecca about what was going on.

He met her at the door with a big kiss and a bag of Chinese food. He asked her to open a bottle of wine because he had some news and wanted to talk to her about it.

Rebecca could see the light in his eyes as he told her what he had heard on the radio. She could feel his excitement as he talked about the possibility of returning to the military. It would mean moving away from Saskatchewan and he wanted to hear what Rebecca thought about it.

It was scary and exciting all at the same time for Rebecca. She hadn't thought of ever leaving the prairies, but here it was. She had hundreds of questions for him over the weekend and Tony tried to answer them the best he could. He tried to dispel any fears she had and said "Rebecca we can do this. It's going to be quite an adventure, something you have never experienced before, but we will be together and we will be secure. The military takes care of their own."

They talked about it all weekend and Sunday afternoon Rebecca came into the kitchen with one last question. She came over and sat at the table next to him. Tony was deep in thought, sipping coffee. "What about the police department application?" she asked. "Do you think it's still possible?"

Tony thought it over for a long time before answering. "I don't know," he sighed. "I just don't know."

She reached over and put her hand over his and looked at him lovingly. "What does your gut tell you to do Tony?" Rebecca asked.

"I want to re-enlist, Rebecca. I want to go back to what I know I can do well."

Rebecca sat back in her chair and put both of her hands palms down on the table. "That's it then, let's do it," she nodded. "Tomorrow is Monday; tomorrow you go down and get your life back."

Bright and early Monday morning Tony found himself walking into the recruiting office and up to the desk. The

Sergeant in Charge looked up at him questioningly. "Can I help you sir?"

"My name is Tony Simons and I'm here to get my life back." The Sergeant looked at him and smiled. An hour later Tony left the recruiting office with a profound sense of pride about himself and he had Travel Orders in his hands. Now he had to tell Rebecca the news. He was leaving Friday for North Bay. Everything would start moving a lot faster and there were many moving parts to this scenario. He was leaving quickly. Rebecca would have to stay behind and sell the house and have it packed up so the military could move the contents to North Bay. Rebecca would be flying, another first.

Before heading home to Rebecca he stopped at his old office and resigned on the spot. He thought he would get a reaction but he didn't. They took his letter and wished him well.

Back home, he broke the news to Rebecca and he could see her eyes widen. "Christ Tony," she gasped, "that's really fast. Are you sure we can do this?"

Tony assured her that it would fall into place and the military would take care of the move.

Tony would help her set up a realtor before he left and he looked at her with concern because he understood this would not be a walk in the park. She would have to stay and make all the necessary preparations for moving on her own, along with that she would have to leave her job once more and meet him in North Bay.

That afternoon Keith phoned Tony to tell him that he too had re-enlisted and was also heading to North Bay and his younger sister would be staying with his older sister, Margaret.

The next morning Tony received a letter from the Regina City Police saying that his application was accepted. He shook his head in disbelief.

The rest of the week was a tailspin of activity; putting the house on the market, setting up movers and finally kissing Rebecca goodbye at the airport with promises of being together again as soon as possible.

Chapter 39

Being back in the military was like he had never left. "The Hole" which was the complex's nickname hadn't changed and the people that worked there ribbed him unmercifully for the next two weeks for leaving in the first place.

Base North Bay was the home of 22nd NORAD Command Region Headquarters. It was in charge of the defence of the North American Airspace from any foreign acts of aggression and unknown aircraft entering Canadian Airspace. It was located just outside the town of North Bay, Ontario in an underground facility, referred to as "the hole."

The Command Centre was accessed through a small portal down a narrow road that crazy bus drivers barreled down at breakneck speeds, sometimes barely missing the walls on either side. At the bottom of the run the bus would stop at the portal controlled by a massive door around three feet thick that you could move with your finger.

Once open, two armed guards were stationed there with submachine guns. When the door was closed, it was impossible to enter the complex. The portal opening was the only way in or out.

Tony was not a stranger to the complex. He had come to North Bay to train many times during his stay in Kamloops.

This was where it all happened. At times, hundreds of men and women in darkened rooms would be watching pale green screens looking for unknown aircraft that might pose a threat to Canada.

Different activities were carried on in other rooms, all with one thing in mind, defend Canadian airspace. It was always a beehive of activity and was located a mile and a half below ground.

Eventually Tony got back up to speed and started to excel. He wanted more and he let his bosses know that he was looking for more diverse challenges.

The house in Regina finally sold and Rebecca joined Tony in North Bay to start their military adventure together.

Chapter 40

Rebecca got off the plane in North Bay to start a strange new life.

Tony was there to greet her and he hugged and kissed her, making her feel that everything was going to be great. He took her by the hand and led her to their car. He then drove them to their apartment. This was where they would be until a PMQ (Private Married Quarters) would be available and their furniture arrived from Saskatchewan.

After owning a house, the apartment wasn't much. It was old and very lived in. But Tony was there and that's all she cared about.

One night after Tony was at work and the boxes had arrived, Rebecca was in the kitchen unpacking dishes. It was getting dark and she looked out the window to see hundreds or even thousands of what she would learn later, were Shadflies on the glass.

North Bay is built along a lake and every year for about three weeks the Shadflies came off the lake and covered everything; neon lights, windows, and streetlights. They only lived for about three weeks and when they died they'd fall onto the sidewalks and streets and made an eerie crunching noise as you walked. Rebecca was disgusted.

A few months later, they moved into a PMQ.

Tony was familiar with PMQ's, he knew people that had lived in them in Kamloops. These were housing units that were owned by the Base, on or off the property that were offered to married personnel at a reduced rate of rent so they could afford housing. It was greatly appreciated by the military members living in them and they were made available to all ranks. Even the Base Commander could apply.

Normally these units were small A-frame, single unit houses, duplexes or row houses consisting of six or more units built together. They were allocated by family size and rank, but one thing was the same, they were built too close together and there were no fences to speak of, to separate anyone or anything. You could always look out your kitchen window and see what was happening across the small yard. It was close, real close.

Kids ran wild in the back yards all day long and the young wives visited neighbours and screamed at their monsters for not doing what they were told. There would always be a half dozen of these ladies pregnant and they hung together, thick as thieves and talked about the other wives in the neighbourhood that were trying to get pregnant or weren't trying at all but ended up pregnant to their husband's surprise.

The women ran the PMQs like a big clique and if you weren't on the inside of the group you were sometimes subject to brutal rumours.

The men went to work or to the mess after work to escape the goings on in the PMQ area. At times they got caught up in the chaos of a bored unhappy housewife telling them what was going on or what they had heard from another gossip crow about whose husband or wife was doing who.

To Tony this brought back many memories of the projects where he grew up with row upon row of grey worker-bee houses with backyards full of screaming kids and a never-ending buzz of rumours and late night goings on. Like it was back in Tony's past, it was the same now. Life in the PMQs was never boring.

Unhappy men would drink in the bars or Base Mess and would come home to fight with their wives at all hours in the morning. You couldn't escape it. Hot summer nights with no air-conditioning and windows open, usually gave you more than you cared to know.

It was a fact that military men and women go away on courses and exercises; sometimes for quite awhile. This often times leads to heavy partying away and at home. With this activity eyes begin to wander and possibilities present themselves.

Lonely, unhappy wives would go to the bars looking for young guys they could pick up and escape their situation for awhile, when their men were away. Other ladies were more ingenious and had devised a code that quietly got around to the single and married guys alike, the OMO box; the unspoken legend in the military.

Everyone knew what it was, but nobody said anything because it wasn't your business. The OMO box (a laundry detergent), also meant "old man out." It was placed in the kitchen window. This was a quiet call in the night from unhappy PMQ wives that they were looking for more than what they were getting at home and this was an opportunity for young males to call.

Tony and Rebecca managed to avoid most of this chaos, but at times it had a way of getting in your face.

Chapter 41

Tony and Rebecca moved into their PMQ. It was a two-storey townhouse type of building. This kind of life was different for Rebecca. She was introduced to friends that Tony knew from the last time he had been in the military, as well as Keith.

It was here that Rebecca learned about the OMO boxes and how, when spouses went on exercises some of the spouses left behind felt that their needs had to be fulfilled by someone else. Rebecca couldn't believe it.

She found temporary work, but before long it was time to leave. They were posted.

Chapter 42

When an opportunity presents itself, you either jump on it or pass and wait for another that may never come.

Tony never let a chance to improve go by. When the boss offered him the opportunity to take a course that was just outside and to the left of what he was doing, he jumped at it.

Tony's boss, Chief Robb, was talking about Base Borden in Ontario and an NBCD (Nuclear, Biological, Chemical, and Defence) Course.

North America and Canada were in a cold war with Russia and part of the training for this was the NBCD courses. There were 14 courses in this field and Tony was being offered one of them. He jumped at it!

He read up on the course before attending and was surprised to find that his trade, AD Tech was deeply involved in this field and could be found on most Bases as part of the BDF (Base Defence Force). This was a cell that was responsible for training Base personnel in weapons, Base Defence and in times of aggression, manning the nuclear shelters during attacks. Once the course was completed Tony would be eligible for a BDF position. In this position he would be involved in survey work after a nuclear explosion or chemical attack, charting blast areas and safe routes around the contaminated areas along with decontamination.

This seemed to be right up Tony's alley. He would get the best of both worlds. He would be outside again; just like in Cornwallis, running through the woods with maps and compass, shooting his rifle and working in a bunkered shelter during exercise, plotting a nuclear attack! What could be better?

The course proved to be exactly what Tony had wanted the military to be for him. Base Borden's NBCD Training School had everything Tony wished for and he was back in combats!

The school lounge was very old and steeped in tradition. It had over-stuffed chairs and couches, a fully-stocked bar, a huge stone fireplace that burned brightly and pictures on the wall of hundreds of courses that had gone through the training years before Tony was born. To him this was what it was all about, the history; he wanted to be part of the history.

He couldn't wait to get back to Rebecca to tell her what a great time he had had.

Once he returned they settled back into military life in the "Bay."

Tony did his best to stay focused on his work but he kept thinking of Borden and the training school. Tony became quite knowledgeable in his section and built a Radar Equipment Training Schedule for all the Bases across Canada. It was noticed and appreciated by his superiors. It wasn't long after that Tony received a call from his boss and was asked if he was interested in an NBC position at CFB Winnipeg, Transport Command.

It would not only be an operational position but a training position as well. He jumped at the opportunity and so began the adventure of a life time for this poor boy from Port Nichols, Ontario and his new wide-eyed bride.

Chapter 43

Tony and Rebecca bought a house a few miles from the Base to avoid the PMQs and Tony settled into his new job easily. He was part of the Base Operations Training Cell along with a Warrant Officer, who was also an AD Tech, there were three others; a Sergeant, Master Corporal and a Corporal, all Army.

They were in charge of Base Defence Training and Tony and the Warrant Officer were responsible for training the Base in Nuclear Defence and shelter duties. Common duties for all five personnel were weapons training and Base qualifications. This was some of Tony's most enjoyable times, being on the ranges, eating in the field and training for Nuclear Emergencies with his team.

Tony got back to Borden many times and took numerous courses dealing with NBCD and First Aid. It was nothing like North Bay or Kamloops and Tony liked it that way. They say that if you like what you are doing it's hard to call it work and that's how Tony felt about Winnipeg.

He was always trying to do his best and it was noticed more and more by the people around him and it paid off with Tony being promoted to Master Corporal and given his own team to train. He kept hearing his boss from North Bay saying to him "don't stay away too long, Simons, it's bad for promotions to be out of trade."

Tony proved him wrong. He was on cloud 9 but it was only going to get better for the Simons family. Three years into the posting Rebecca and Tony found out they were going to have a baby.

Chapter 44

Tony and Rebecca could have done the "At Home Test," but they had had a false alarm previously so this time Rebecca headed over to her doctor's office before going to work and left a urine sample. She was told that she would get a call with the results.

Rebecca was nervous all day and at about 2 in the afternoon the phone finally rang. She answered immediately and a voice on the other end told her that it was the doctor's office calling with her results. Rebecca held her breath and the nurse said "it's positive."

Rebecca couldn't speak for a moment and then she finally said "what do I do now?"

The nurse laughed and told her she needed to make an appointment with her doctor.

She took a few minutes to calm herself before calling Tony. "How could two little words change her whole life?" "It's positive."

She called Tony and he answered with "well?"

She took a deep breath and said "it's positive Tony!"

Tony's whole world turned upside down. At first he was scared, then happy and then he was scared again. He couldn't imagine what Rebecca was going through. He had to be strong and be there for her.

Time seemed to fly in Winnipeg and so did Rebecca's pregnancy. As fate usually does, it stepped in again and Tony and Rebecca were transferred to Cold Lake, Alberta. This time, there was a problem. There were no PMQs available and no affordable housing to be purchased. Tony was put on a waiting list for a PMQ.

With Rebecca's due date getting closer and the move even closer, Tony asked the Section Commander at his new unit if Rebecca could wait out the time at her mother's house in Saskatoon, and he would move into barracks until a PMQ was available.

It would be much easier on Rebecca to be with her mother as she had not been feeling well and Tony didn't want her staying in a motel in the Cold Lake area while he went to work. The request was granted and Rebecca went back to Saskatoon, while Tony went to Cold Lake.

A few months later, Tony was finally given a PMQ. Rebecca joined him immediately.

The house was a pre-war A-frame style building with two small bedrooms upstairs that had slanting walls and small windows.

It wasn't long after that the Simonses welcomed a wonderful addition, a beautiful baby girl who they named "Sadie."

Sadie was the best thing that ever happened to Tony and Rebecca. She turned their world upside down in a wonderful way and gave new meaning to the 2400 hour clock. Sadie was all day, every day and tested the new parents' endurance. It was amazing to say the least.

Every day was a learning curve and they would not have wanted it any other way.

Tony's new job was to become the most challenging time in his military career. He was in a two man section, Tony and his boss, an officer with 27 years in. He was an ex navigator named Sherman that was riding his time out trying not to make any waves and he drank like a fish.

Sherman was an educated drunk and knew when and when not to hit the bottle. He only drank vodka or white rum straight so as to hide the smell. He would get drunk at the Officers' Mess and phone Tony at home at all hours to come and pick him up or to borrow money because he was broke.

Sherman was rarely in the office, but when he was, he was off visiting with someone or another. Tony was left to figure out the section's role in Base Exercises and train their personnel in shelter operations, along with decontamination of personnel and aircraft.

Only months into the posting at Cold Lake, Tony got a call from Flight Commander Tally. He told Tony that Sherman had suffered a massive heart attack at his home and passed away.

Tony went to work the next day and sat at his desk looking at Sherman's empty chair. Plenty of people came by over the next week or so and gave Tony their condolences and told him to ask if he needed anything. He would say thanks but he'd be ok.

Tony was called into the Flight Commander's Office a week or so after Sherman was buried and he was advised that there would be no replacement for some time. Tally wanted to know if Tony could handle the job.

Tony assured him that things would be fine and the Base training would continue. Tally advised him that the Base's Tactical Evaluation was still a year away and he was sure that a replacement could be found for Sherman and his role as the Base Nuclear Defence Officer and Radiation Specialist.

Tony took on this challenge with a vengeance. He learned how to write a Nuclear Exercise complete with radiation fallout and aircraft decontamination. He got the Base Hospital to participate in mass casualty exercises, and the Base Kitchen to setup for fourteen days of lockdown survival.

Chapter 45

This was Rebecca's second experience with PMQ life. Since she wouldn't be working right away, she thought she'd settle in and get to know some of the other ladies in the neighbourhood.

Josie, one of her neighbours, seemed friendly enough but she was much younger than Rebecca who was having her first child at 32. Josie had just had her sixth child!

Josie's husband was a long-time Private with a temper and couldn't keep his hands off his wife, and as Rebecca heard, off of other wives as well.

Rebecca's other neighbour was Ramona. She was closer to Rebecca's age and had two children. Her husband was a Corporal.

Rebecca was still new to PMQ living and military life in general. She was unaware of the workings of the rank system as it pertained to the wives. She thought now that

Sadie had come along she'd be welcomed into the "mom club."

It wasn't to happen. Rebecca was an older, new mom; she was new to the PMQ area and she'd always worked. Rebecca's husband was a Master Corporal and most of the other women in the area were married to Privates and Corporals, had never worked, had many children and wore their husband's rank.

Rebecca was different, so while she stayed at home she devoted her time to Sadie and Tony and eventually started working again, this time with the military. It would give her a better understanding of Tony's work and she would learn "the military language."

Chapter 46

Time was moving on and the Evaluation was getting closer with no replacement for Sherman in sight. Tally called Tony into his office and broke the news. There would be no replacement for Sherman in time for the Base Evaluation.

Tony did not bat an eye, he could do this. Tally told him that the Base was in dire need of a Radiation Safety Officer and there were none to be had. He asked Tony how his math was and if he thought he could pass the course in Borden and take over the responsibilities of the Base Radiation Safety Officer during the Evaluation.

Tony reminded the Commander that this course was for officers only and he was a Master Corporal. Tally said he had some pull at the school and could get him in, but he would be alone after hours in another barracks so studying would be difficult. If he accepted he had to pass the course.

Tony accepted the challenge and two days later he found himself back in Borden taking a course he never thought he could.

He sat by himself in the back of the classroom and toughed out five weeks of intense training. He graduated with a "B." It was a solid "B" and Tony was very proud of his accomplishment.

Back at the Base he presented the Flight Commander with his scroll. Tally beamed and shook Tony's hand. A message went out to all Base Personnel and Section Heads that the new Radiation Safety Officer at Base Cold Lake was indeed Master Corporal Tony Simons and in that capacity he was to be shown every courtesy.

Tony received numerous visitors and calls of congratulations, but the Base Evaluation was getting closer so the exercises had to step up.

Tony was once again called into Tally's office and asked to sit down. It had come to his attention that the Base had no Evacuation Policy or Procedures in Times of Aggression under Nuclear Attack. Sherman had not produced one.

Tony assured the Flight Commander that he could indeed produce a plan, but it would take input from the entire Base if he called on them for help.

Three weeks later and after many meetings and planning sessions, Tony handed over a complete Evacuation Procedure that contained everything needed to move the entire Base, 500 miles away, complete with hospital, kitchen, operational staff and shelters; but most importantly, fighter aircraft.

The Base Evaluation went off without a hitch and Tony received the Base Commander's Commendation for all his work. Shortly after, he was promoted to Sergeant.

Chapter 47

Life for the Simons family was moving along pretty well. Tony loved his job and at home he and Rebecca were head over heels in love with Sadie. She was growing like a weed and getting into everything because that's what two year olds do.

Tony knew that their time in Cold Lake was nearing an end and wanted to continue the adventure that was his career. There was only one place that could do that for them and that was Germany. He put in his request and it was granted.

The Simons family was moving to Europe!

Tony, Rebecca and Sadie were off to Lahr, Germany. This was an Army Base located in the southern most part of Germany known as the Black Forrest. It was five minutes from France and fifteen minutes from Switzerland. The area was "old Germany." It was beautiful in every way and covered with forests and farmland.

The flight over was made at night and took forever. Sadie's ears were bothering her badly and with nothing they could do, it made the trip even longer. Eight long hours later, Tony and his tired family landed in Lahr.

The door to the aircraft opened and the first thing Tony saw and experienced was haze and humidity. It was warm in Germany and it rained a lot. The valley that Lahr was situated in gleamed in the morning dew and promised to be a spectacular day.

Before leaving Cold Lake, Tony talked for many hours with his sponsor in Lahr. His name was Randy Moore. They talked about housing, buying a car, and where to shop. All of these questions had been asked and answered years before by thousands of servicemen and their families.

The Base was self-contained with all the amenities you could imagine but military personnel were encouraged to shop on the German economy.

Tony was told that the PMQ situation was not the greatest, but available. They decided to live off Base and surround themselves with the beauty that was Germany.

Randy had found them a beautiful stone house 25 kilometers away from the Base in a village called "Oberhausen." Randy had assured them they would love the place and there were only two other Canadian families living in the village.

Randy loaded the Simons family into his Volkswagen Passat and headed off Base onto the German highway. Welcome to the Autobahn. Tony and Rebecca were not ready for it. Randy accelerated quickly and was up to 160 kms an hour in no time flat. He seemed comfortable at the speed but Rebecca wasn't. Tony could see the terror in her eyes as she held Sadie close.

Tony looked over at Randy with questions in his eyes. "The German highways have no speed limit, Tony, and you have to stay with the flow. It's too dangerous to go slower. It's really easy once you get used to it. I've got to show you something though," he said slowly. "There's a vehicle coming up behind us, Watch straight ahead, Tony, you're not going to believe it when it passes us."

Tony didn't know what he was talking about; all he could see was highway and farmland. It happened so fast, Tony wasn't ready and couldn't believe it when it happened. In less than a second a black Lamborghini shot by them but Tony only had time to catch a glimpse of the beautiful woman driving it. "What the hell?" he asked.

"Told you Tony, no speed limits," Randy replied. "If you drive in the left hand lane, you have to keep one eye in your rearview mirror. Watch for flashing lights coming up behind you, if you see them, get back in the right lane and let them pass because they will pass you no matter what."

The rest of the drive was uneventful, but the experience with the Lamborghini was a lesson learned.

Randy finally pulled off the Autobahn and went down a secondary road to pull into the small town of Oberhausen. The houses were hundreds of years old and mostly made of stone or old wood. The roads were made of cobblestone. There was a bank, a few small shops, a pub or what Tony would find out later was a "Gasthaus," and a small Town Hall, all visible from the street. For the most part, everything else was set back and very quiet.

Randy made a left turn down a quiet street and at the end of a short road, just before the farmland took over, was their new home.

It was a beautiful two story stone building, quite new in comparison to the rest of the buildings. It had a wrap around balcony and large windows on every side of the structure. The house was painted white and had heavy oak doors leading inside.

The place was massive and Tony and Rebecca would have to furnish it fast, but for now, just opening the windows and letting a slight breeze move through was enough.

Tony didn't have to report to work for three more days and there were things he needed to do before they could move into their new home.

Randy had checked them into the Base Hotel or "temporary housing," as it was known and picked him up the next day so he could write his driver's license test and buy a car. He had been studying the book for some time so the test and all the new road signs came easy.

Tony managed to pick up a used Volkswagen that ran well for a fare price and he drove back to pick up Rebecca. They bought some furnishings from the Base CANEX and had them delivered and they moved into their new home the next day.

Tony reported into Base Operations and was introduced to his training section by his boss, a Warrant Officer named Randy Moore. It was, as Tony knew it would be; a full training section responsible for shelters or CMPs (Canadian Modular Protection) as they were called. They were large submarine-like tubes, buried half way into the ground and could hold a hundred men for fourteen days.

They had NBC responsibility of two WOCs, (Wartime Operation Centres) which were the Command Centres during any nuclear or chemical activity. Of course Tony was responsible for the gas hut training, which was his favourite.

Working with Base Operations was like a dream come true for Tony, but the best part was when he was asked to become part of NATO's (North Atlantic Treaty Organization) Tactical Evaluation Team. This was a group of skilled military men from all over Europe that were tasked with evaluating the NATO Alliance Bases in their ability to survive a nuclear or chemical attack.

At this time Tony thought he had reached his peak. He had a great job and a great place to live. Tony, Rebecca and Sadie settled right into their home in Oberhausen.

Chapter 48

The old town of Oberhausen had rules that everyone complied with and this included the Simons family. They had to recycle and no one worked on Sundays and no one hung their laundry outside. You only realize just how much you usually do on Sunday when you're not allowed to do it.

Oberhausen was very quiet and everyone kept to themselves. The neighbours across the street saw that the Simonses had a young girl they were raising and that changed everything. The Germans love children and took to Sadie right away. They were great people that went out of their way to welcome the Simons family to their little town and to ensure they experienced a true German way of life.

Willy, Hedrick and Anja lived in a very old stone house with an old courtyard and barn just across the street. Willy had long since retired because of an industrial accident he had had many years before and Hedrick was like the grandma you always wanted. She never stopped smiling and could always be found in her kitchen wearing the same old apron.

Their home was very tiny but they loved it because it was their own. Tony was sure that they were both pensioned off but that it brought them very little money. To subsidize their income Willy raised rabbits for meat which he sold in the market. He let them roam free in his field and watched them from a camouflaged shed.

Willy would sit in the shed most of the day with his best friend Dieter, drinking beer, talking and watching the rabbits, which Willy protected. This was not only a great place to drink beer, but it was out of the watchful eye of Hedrick.

The town had plenty of feral cats. They were cats that had gone wild and they loved to kill rabbits for food. They were Willy's sworn enemies and he killed as many as he could.

Since the war, German's were not allowed to own guns unless they were part of a hunting club. Willy was not allowed to own a rifle but he did have a pellet gun. This gun, Dieter modified by hooking it up to a high powered compressor and mounted an eight times scope on it which Willy mounted onto a tripod. He could scan the entire four acres with deadly accuracy. If Willy saw a cat enter the field, it was put down immediately and another beer was opened to celebrate.

Tony spent a few days in the shed with the two guys, watching the action and drinking beer for beer with them. That was a mistake. Don't try to keep pace with a hard-core German drinker, you will lose and pay the price.

Sadie loved playing in Willy's courtyard and especially on a little bridge in the courtyard that went over a small creek separating the field from the barn. At the end of the day Willy would have Sadie stand on the bridge and he would whistle loudly into the field. This was a signal to the rabbits that it was supper time for them and to run to the barn.

They would hear the whistle and would all race into the courtyard at once trying to get over the bridge with Sadie in the middle of it. It was quite a sight and she loved it and it made her giggle. Sadie didn't know at the time, but the race to the bridge for the rabbits had a secondary incentive; the last rabbit to cross the bridge was that night's supper!

It was just one of the many things Tony and Rebecca learned or experienced during the first three years of living in Germany.

Oberhausen was located right in the middle of the Black Forrest and had hundreds of years of tradition to look back on. The people who lived in the village were farmers. Their fathers were farmers and their fathers' fathers before them. They were proud of their village and respected the traditions of the past. One of these traditions that Tony experienced was the local Gasthaus, or pub. There was more than one in the tiny village but one thing that was always the same in all of them, was the "locals' table." It was easy to spot when you entered the door. It had no tablecloth on it and the only thing on the table was a huge old ashtray and a pot of warm water. The water was for beer. The German's liked their beer at room temperature.

It was considered an honour if a seat at the table was offered to sit and chat. It was not offered lightly. If you weren't asked to sit, you stayed away.

When you entered the Gasthaus it was like stepping back in time, there were old tables and chairs, checkered window coverings, antlers hanging on the walls and a heavy pipe smell that permeated everywhere. It was usually quiet during the week except for the retired local farmers that liked to come for beer and conversation.

The Simons family experienced many of the German traditions in Oberhausen; "Fasching," which was a carnival time where the different villages dressed in their guild costumes and had parades; "Hexennacht," or the burning of the witch; "Oktoberfest," which included music, dance, food and much beer! Christmas time was an amazing time of the year, from the markets in Lahr to the Christmas villages in the mountains, everyone celebrated!

Chapter 49

The Simons family was having the time of their lives; but things were changing at work. There was tension in the air as Europe was sensing trouble in the Middle East. On August 2, 1990 a madman from Iraq named Saddam Hussein invaded Kuwait and confiscated all the oil rich lands in the Persian Gulf area. This did not go unanswered by the United Nations and a huge coalition force led by the United States, known as Desert Storm, prepared to march against Saddam and his Iraqi armies.

Troops from many nations were being sent to forward locations in the Persian Gulf to set up strike camps in the event of war. The Canadians in Lahr were no exception. Two forward camps were located south of Bagdad in a small state called Qatar. More precisely, a city called Doha, just outside of Bahrain. This location was to be the Canadian Air Force Headquarters and forward strike area if needed. It was well within Saddam's missile strike zone. This was the start of Operation Friction which was Canada's contribution to the coalition forces.

Tony was well aware of what was going on and was watching it closely. He had been training Base personnel steadily for the last month or so to be deployed to Doha and knew his time was coming quickly.

There was a lot of talk about weapons of mass destruction being used, but the big eye-opener for Tony was the talk of chemical weapons already being used on civilians.

More and more information was coming out of Qatar and more and more military personnel were being retrained in chemical defence and mask drills. Doha now had two NBC personnel and an Officer in camp. The officer was a friend of Tony's named Lou Tanner. The task of setting up and training was too much for them. Adding additional NBC personnel was the only answer.

All the years of training and teaching was finally going to be put to the test. On Friday afternoon, December 28, Tony was called into the Flight Commander's office. Colonel Wayne Talbot advised him that he would be leaving for the Persian Gulf in one week.

"Are there any questions?" the Flight Commander asked.

"No, sir" Tony quickly replied. He walked out of the Commander's office, adrenalin pumping in his veins and his mind spinning faster than a turbine. He was going to Qatar!

Tony left the Flight Commander's office and reported to Randy Moore, his Section Supervisor and told him what had just happened. Unknown to Tony, Randy already knew what was going on but let Tony explain wide-eyed and out of breath.

It was near the end of the day and Tony asked to leave early so he could pick up Rebecca at the Headquarters and Sadie at the sitter for the ride home.

Chapter 50

Charles Dickens wrote "It was the best of times; it was the worst of times." Rebecca felt she knew just what that meant.

Moving to Germany was exciting and scary all at the same time. She was a small town prairie girl after all. Oh the country was beautiful; the house that their sponsors had picked out for them was equally as beautiful as was the village they lived in.

It was hard navigating the language barrier, but the people were friendly and helpful. They loved children. It was hard teaching Sadie to be wary of strangers while frequently being stopped by a sweet "Oma" ogling her, saying what a sweet, pretty, little girl she was and handing her chocolate!

Not long after they had settled into their home in Germany, Rebecca got word that her mother was ill and soon after passed. She had to leave Sadie with their sponsors, now friends, for a week while she returned to Canada to help bury her and sort her belongings.

Still addled with grief she returned to Germany to find she had been accepted into a position with the Army Brigade. She had to find childcare for Sadie quickly.

Tony was engulfed in his work and the Simons family settled into a routine. They travelled the surrounding countries and met dozens of wonderful people.

Their happiness was shattered by tension in Europe brought on by someone in the Middle East called "Saddam."

Rebecca got rumbles from Tony at home and from the military personnel she worked with.

Finally, the Americans gave Saddam an ultimatum. Nerves were on edge.

Sadie, now attending kindergarten on the Base went to and from school on a Bus, only now there were soldiers with guns along for the ride to keep the children safe. Before entering the Base all vehicles were checked and rods with mirrors were slid under them, checking for bombs!

Rebecca could see that Tony was worried, but there was word around her work that the Army would be deployed and not the Air Force.

Chapter 51

Rebecca, in her position with the Army Brigade in the Canadian Headquarters building was fully aware of what was happening in Qatar, it was abuzz all over the Headquarters.

Rebecca knew Lou Tanner, Tony's friend and also knew that he was the Captain in charge of NBC and was already there with two Corporals, overwhelmed with work that had to be done. She knew it would only be a matter of time before the bosses would be looking at Tony and she was dreading that day.

The rumour mill about what was happening in the Persian Gulf was truly running wild and Rebecca could feel tension in the air at work.

The United Nations had finally given Saddam a deadline to remove his troops from Kuwait, January 15, 1991.

The Canadian Headquarters was a madhouse of activity. Rebecca finally finished work and stepped out of the building to get a breath of fresh air and wait for Tony. To her surprise he was already in the parking lot, waiting for her.

He was leaning on the back trunk of the Jetta and as she got closer, he straightened up and started ringing his hands together. He was staring right at her with what she knew as his "military eyes." It was his serious look. He didn't have to say a thing, she knew. A sick feeling was welling up in her stomach and her body tensed.

She came toward him quickly and threw her arms around his neck, burying her face in his chest. "When are you leaving?" she asked.

Tony felt like he had been struck by lightning, "how did she know?" he thought.

He wrapped his arms around her lovingly and answered her quietly "next Friday, babe, Saturday at the latest."

"I knew it," she said, "just by the way you were looking at me."

"You have to promise me you're going to be careful, Tony," she said as her voice started to break up and tears started to roll down her cheeks, "you have to."

"I won't do anything that will stop me from getting back to you and Sadie," he answered softly.

The ride back home was very quiet. Both Tony and Rebecca were deep in their own thoughts, but knew they had to talk more about what was coming and soon.

They were inseparable through the New Years' holidays and talked for hours on end about things they had to do now and what they could do when Tony got back.

They phoned the family back home to let them know what was happening and got the same reaction, disbelief, panic and then resolve. Again Tony promised to stay safe and try to stay in touch.

A holiday was definitely in their plans and Rebecca was going to make it happen as soon as he got back. She kept saying "it's going to be epic, Tony, just wait and see."

She put on a brave front but Tony could see the strain in her face and knew she wasn't sleeping well. Because of the holidays, work started up on Tuesday with Tony receiving his Travel Orders. Saturday, 1400 hours was his flight time.

The rest of the work week was a blur of briefings and being kitted for the desert, another medical, a million needles and it was Friday.

Rebecca found it hard to understand why the officers in the Army Brigade Headquarters where she worked seemed disappointed that they hadn't been deployed. Tony explained that this is what soldiers, no matter what their discipline, trained for and most of them wanted to experience it.

Chapter 52

After a long sleepless night, with Sadie in his arms and Rebecca at his side they walked into the AMU to wait for his plane. Tony's mind was swimming with questions he kept asking himself; "am I prepared for this? Will I get back in one piece? Would Rebecca be alright? What if either Sadie or Rebecca gets sick? Jesus, what if I get sick?" He had to give himself a shake and snap out of it.

The Hercules landed and rolled up to the AMU. Tony turned to Rebecca one more time and pulled her into his arms to kiss her. "I'll be back, babe," he said "I promise." He lifted Sadie into his arms and kissed her on the cheek. "Take care of mommy," he said. Sadie just looked at him. He handed her to Rebecca and hugged them both tightly.

"You get your ass back here as soon as you can," she said. "You have people here that love you."

Tony gave her a slight smile and a wink, turned away and headed for the aircraft.

Tony left for a place Rebecca had never heard of before – The Persian Gulf. After tear-filled goodbyes, and when they could no longer see the plane, they left the airfield.

Chapter 53

The flight from Lahr to Doha took 12 hours but Tony saw some of the most beautiful scenery he had seen in his life. It was 0200 on Sunday morning January 6, 1991 and Tony found it hard to believe that a hard luck kid from Port Nichols, Ontario landed in the Persian Gulf amidst tension he had never experienced before.

The runway lights were turned off just as the plane stopped so as not to draw attention to it. The cargo door opened and dropped to the ground and Tony was immediately greeted by very warm, dry heat and a brisk wind. He grabbed his bag and walked down the ramp into the Persian Gulf night.

He wasn't sure what to expect but he wasn't going to be caught in the open in the middle of the night. There wasn't one light on. It was darker than dark. Tony's eyes started to become adjusted to his surroundings when out of the corner of his eye, just over to the right of a blackened building, he saw a light blinking intermittently. He crouched down, not sure what to make of it, and waited. There was nothing, just the dark, the wind and the blinking light.

Tony decided to take his chances and head toward the light. He started to make his way across the tarmac, staying as low as he could, moving as quickly as he could. Finally at about twenty five yards he recognized a Tilley hat and underneath it was a familiar face, Lou Tanner.

Tony moved toward him and tried to give him a salute. Lou caught his arm in mid-stride and whispered "we don't salute people here Tony, it makes for targets."

That was Tony's first and last mistake. From now on, he'd be on guard.

Lou Tanner took Tony to his trailer and gave him the top bunk to sleep in until his spot was available. "Sleep if you can," he said, "tomorrow is a big day."

Sleep was not an option for Tony, all he could think of was "Jesus, I'm in Saudi Arabia, what the hell am I doing in Saudi Arabia."

The sun rises early in the desert and Tony had boots on the ground at 0500. When he opened the trailer door his eyes were immediately assaulted by the intense sunlight and constant wind. His new home was nothing more than a group of trailers surrounded by barbed wire, sandbags and men with guns, lots of guns.

Lou took Tony around the camp known as "CD2" (Canadian Depot) to clear-in, get his briefings, and finally receive his Tilley Hat. It had a very wide brim and would help keep the sun from blinding him. "Always have it with you," Lou said, "and your sunglasses too. Stay sharp, be aware and always have your mask with you."

"Words to live by," Tony said.

The camp had locals working inside the fence doing the mundane jobs that needed to be accomplished on a day to day basis, cleaning mostly. Tony was very much aware of them and didn't like it when they got close. They were quiet, very dark eyed and always watching. It made for a long day.

It was 2245 before Tony got to his bunk and found Lou waiting for him. As he sat down on his bed, Lou gave him a field message pad and a pen. "This is something we've never done before, Tony," Lou said. "Every night, take a minute and write what happened to you during the day. It's important that you journal what's happening here."

Chapter 54

It was nine days until the deadline the UN had given Saddam.

The next day was the same for Tony, weapons orientation and hard work trying to get the camp ready for whatever was to come.

The newspapers were not very encouraging; eight days left. The camp was getting bigger, more men, more equipment and more planes from all the coalition forces in the campaign. All were armed and ready to strike. Stress was starting to show in the camp, tempers were short and things were getting out of hand quickly. The work was never ending, but Tony could see progress.

The American forces had been there longer than the Canadians and Tony wanted to see how they were set up. To his surprise, the American camp was abuzz with things to do, basketball, arcade games, a movie tent and a CANEX store where you could purchase just about everything. "Heaven in the desert," Tony thought.

In his borrowed bunk that night, Tony found himself thinking about Rebecca and Sadie. They were so far away.

"Tony," Lou said "tomorrow you and I are going to drive into Doha so you can get the lay of the land. I'm going to show you where the Canadian Embassy is so you can get there on your own, if necessary."

"What did he mean by that?" Tony thought.

The next day started with high tension in the camp, because of the news that the peace talks had failed and war was imminent. Alert states were going up all around the camp and the airfield.

Lou had asked the guys to meet him at 0900 in the office, which was basically a make-shift shed, so they could talk about it.

When the guys got to the shed, Lou told them to be aware of the people around them at all times. "Don't talk openly about the camp's status. Stay in teams, and keep your masks close."

The camp had not been shut down yet, but they knew it was coming.

Lou and Tony drove into Doha so Tony could get an awareness of his surroundings. He was shown where the Embassy was, and was introduced to the Ambassador and his family.

Tony was still trying to figure out why Lou had taken him there until, while on the way back to camp, he told Tony that they were going to train the Ambassador and his debutante wife in secret, how to mask and suit up during the evening hours prior to the start of the war. Earlier, Lou had been advised that the Ambassador and his wife were not going to leave the Embassy if there were any hostilities, but Lou had convinced them to remove their two children out of the area for safety.

"Holy Christ, Lou!" was all Tony could manage.

For the next two nights they went to the Canadian Embassy and tried to teach them how to survive. The Ambassador took to the training easily, but his debutante wife was another story.

She was a spoiled young woman that had gone to all the best schools, wore the best clothes and was waited on hand and foot. She wasn't ready for the rough green overall that fit her badly, and the mask smelled like something she had never experienced before, rubber. She didn't want it to touch her face, let alone smell it. She was horrified when she broke one of her finely manicured nails and got her hair messed. She nearly fainted when Tony suggested that she put her seven pure-bred Persian cats in cages and use them as chemical sentries outside and around the compound during an attack. He was not joking, the cats went out.

The Ambassador and his family were not alone in the Embassy, they had many servants from in and around Doha and they were watched all the time. A team of highly trained RCMP security was always in sight.

Tony studied the security team as he trained the whining debutante on how to seal her mask. The officers were tall, mid-thirties, muscular and well-dressed. They didn't say much and kept a respectable distance, but Tony could see that they were armed and ready to protect the family. Another thing Tony noticed was that they had military gas masks close by. When the Ambassador needed a break, Tony introduced himself to the nearest agent and asked to inspect his mask.

The Ambassador nodded his head and the agent relaxed a little and handed Tony his mask.

"Like I was saying, my name is Tony Simons, and I am here, as you can see, to train your charges on how to protect themselves."

The officer introduced himself as Inspector Sam Higgins and his partner on the other side of the room was Inspector Dan Blocker.

Tony looked over and got a nod.

"Can I inspect your mask, sir?" he asked.

The officer looked down at Tony and said "Sam, call me Sam, and please do look at my mask."

As Tony looked hard at the mask, Sam asked him a couple of questions. "You're the specialist that's training the camp, right?" Tony nodded as he continued looking at the mask. "Are you good at what you do?" Sam probed.

Tony looked right at him "I'm the best at what I do." Sam nodded again. "Good, we're going to need you."

Tony stopped what he was doing. He found a problem with Sam's mask. Tony showed him a valve problem inside the mask and corrected it in less than a second, but if left unchecked would have been deadly.

Sam watched the correction and promised Tony that all the officers there would be told about this fix and to check their masks. Sam thanked him and as Tony moved away back to the Ambassador, the agent asked him in a low voice. "Can you save them Specialist?"

"Only if they help themselves," Tony answered and moved away.

Chapter 55

Six days to go. It was a banner day. Tony slept until 0730 and was then shaken back to reality by the headlines on the Stars and Stripes Newsletter. "The 11th Hour has passed!" it read.

Tony shook his head, "now isn't that inspiring?" he said to himself.

He headed to the mess tent and noted that the camp was now full of reporters from all over the world. They had come to see the show. How they had gotten there was anybody's guess. One thing was for sure, they were interviewing anyone they could.

Tony tried to avoid them and go about his work by visiting the other camp but was shaken to the very core when an air raid siren went off as he entered the gate and everybody dove for cover into the sandbag shelters.

Tony was in his suit and mask faster than anytime he had tried before. He never found out what the problem was but stayed in the hole for many hours until the "all clear" siren was sounded.

Lou got word that many Embassies in Doha were closing and more and more people were crowding to the airport, trying to escape. A lot of them wouldn't get out. Word was that the civilian airport would be closed the next morning.

Chapter 56

Four more days to go; Tony was up at 0800. It was his first day off and he wanted to make the most of it.

Avoiding the reporters, he managed to drive out the gate with a few friends in tow. They went down into Doha, only to find that the city was under strict martial law. Nothing moved without being checked, including Tony and his friends.

They were advised by the police that taking pictures was strictly forbidden and if caught doing so, they would be visiting the inside of a Qatari prison. That got their attention, so they left Doha and drove out into the desert to chase a few filthy camels and watch a desert golf course in action.

People were actually carrying a one by one piece of Astroturf to hit the ball off of and putt on a concrete surface covered with the same.

The guys drove back to the outskirts of Doha to look for a Souk or market to buy treasures to send home.

The market they found was a maze of people with covered faces, camels, dogs and children begging from passersby, dozens of them.

The spookiest thing that bothered Tony the most was the women. They were all dressed in black from head to toe. The only thing you could see were their dark eyes looking back at you from behind a veil or their heavily decorated hands darting out from behind their clothing as they made deals.

Tony had been in the region a week by then, but they still made him nervous. "I hate it when the kids come up behind you to beg," Tony said to his friend.

They found a Stars and Stripes Newspaper in one of the shops and read the headline, "SADDAM HAS NO CHOICE, LEAVE NOW!"

Tony knew that a lot of people wanted this crazy man out of Kuwait, Tony wasn't any different, but it wasn't looking good.

Once the guys made a few purchases, it was time to drive back to the camp. Late that afternoon, Lou told his team that the Americans had raised their threat levels and were preparing to strike and liberate the oilfields in the Qatar state and confront the Iranians in the desert. This was bad news!

The guys agreed to sleep with their clothes on, masks close by and in shifts to lower the stress.

A new worker, Terry Johns was coming in that night at 0200 and Tony was to be there to pick him up, but he didn't show. He had been delayed on route somewhere.

Chapter 57

Three days left. The day began at 0500, only this time with a twist. The camp had been ordered to make ready to evacuate.

Tony wasn't sure what was going on, but his section would be ready, even if nothing happened.

Camp security had found a second location where the Base could operate from if the need was there. The jets would fly to other unknown airstrips.

This activity was driving the reporters into frenzy and the need for them to get a story was causing concern. They were lurking everywhere or getting into people's faces, trying to find out what was going on. It made things even worse when Lou called Tony into his office and told him they would be going back to the Embassy and he was to take as many gas masks as he could fit into the truck.

Along the way Lou told Tony they were going to try and mask as many Canadians that worked in the Embassy and the surrounding buildings as they could that had not made it out before the airport closed. This would also include their families.

"Oh my god Lou!" Tony shrieked, as he shook his head. "That's going to start a panic if this gets out!"

There was no keeping this activity quiet, the Embassy was already crawling with reporters and it was like feeding time at the zoo when Lou and Tony rolled up and started off-loading the boxes.

The Ambassador tried to explain to the reporters that this was a precautionary measure only but they were having none of it. To the reporters this was the Canadian Embassy preparing for a chemical attack.

It was bad enough trying to teach mask and fitting drills to around 100 or so frightened civilians with reporters in their faces but what was even worse, was when they wanted their children fitted too.

This drove the press crazy and security tried to contain them.

Tony tried to explain to the people with children that these masks were made for adults and that they would not seal properly on a child's face. Tony was asked to try anyway.

With anguished parents telling their children to be calm and reporters taking pictures of anything that moved, Tony went about the task of trying to fit a gas mask on a scared child that didn't know what was happening. As Tony confirmed, the mask did not fit.

The reporters ate it up and surrounded the parents and the crying child asking them what they were going to do now.

This went on all afternoon with Tony and Lou having some success masking a few older teenagers but the little ones left the area crying in their terrified mother's arms.

The RCMP security detail that Tony had met a day or so earlier, were watching this mayhem from close by and at times caught Tony's eye. They could see that this was affecting him and could tell the stress was unbearable.

They both shook their heads and looked down so as not to see the terror in the young children's faces as the mask was put on, while trying to stay vigilant.

Tony was trying to stay calm as he went about his task, but inside he was raging. "Why the hell were they staying here?" he thought, "and with their children for Christ's sake! Where were their heads? They had waited too long!"

During one of the breaks Tony permitted himself, a civilian came up to him and asked his opinion. "You've made a mistake," Tony said flatly, "you shouldn't be here, and neither should your children."

Shaken by this answer, the man continued. "And why are you here?" his voice was cracking.

Tony answered him as clear and directly as he could, "it's my job!"

Even with all the anarchy going on, it was not going unnoticed by the locals that worked in the huge building. They weren't saying anything, just quietly watching the white foreigners trying to save themselves and their children. If Tony had taken a minute to talk to one of the cleaning ladies, he would have seen the same terror in their eyes as he was seeing in the Canadians he was trying to save.

It had been a very long day and Tony was physically and mentally drained. It was 2200 when he finally climbed into the truck and before he could start the engine, Sam appeared out of nowhere and startled the hell out of him. He came up to the window, bent down and stared at Tony and Lou for a minute.

"You did good today, Specialist," and walked away.

Chapter 58

Tony didn't even remember driving back to the camp, only finally falling into his bunk, exhausted with the visions of frightened, crying children flashing in and out of his memory.

He started to see Sadie's face behind the mask, telling him to stop and crying for Rebecca. Sleep finally released him from his personal hell.

Two days left. Tony woke late, 0800 and wondered why Lou had not gotten him up. He dressed and walked to the mess tent and entered to find Lou with two other NBC guys that had come in late in the night as Tony slept. Lou had picked them up. "The man is a machine," Tony thought to himself. "When does he sleep?" he wondered.

Tony was introduced to Steve Pounds and Terry Sheer. Two names he had heard of before, back home, but had never met.

The two were to complete the compliment of NBC personnel needed and would be housed in a new trailer which was also to be Tony's new home. All Tony could think of was "finally, no top bunk."

Lou asked Tony to clear the new guys in and make the move himself to his new trailer. As Tony got up to leave Lou stopped him at the door and told him that when he was done with the move, he was to take the afternoon off and relax. "Read, listen to music or go over to the American camp and play some arcade games, but no working."

Tony nodded to his friend and boss and headed out the tent to get the new pinkies cleared in and issued their Tilley hats.

With the new help settled in, Tony told them to report to the boss for work assignments and schedules. Then he headed to the truck to get away from the madness, if only for a few hours.

Because anyone leaving the camp could not leave alone, Tony hooked up with a friend of his, Ray Grimes, a Military Policeman and off they went.

With Doha under martial law and everything pretty much shut down, the two friends found themselves on a pier in the downtown harbour, watching the locals navigate their small fishing boats to the docks to offload their catch and head back out into the Persian Gulf, only to be dwarfed in size by the mighty warships that were at harbour waiting for orders. It was quite a contrast.

It was getting late in the afternoon, but the sun was shining brightly and would continue to do so for many more hours. Tony always marveled at this. "What do you want to do Ray?" Tony asked. "It's too early to go back to camp."

His friend pondered the question a minute, finally coming up with a plan. "Let's go down to the Souk," he said, "you know that's open. We can get a bite to eat there and look around for awhile. Maybe you'll find that treasure you've been looking for."

They parked just outside the market, making sure their masks were concealed in their gym bags. Ray was busily looking around, not paying attention, tripped over some decorative pans that were being sold on the ground as they entered the Souk and fell on his ass. His gym bag went flying in the air. When it hit the ground, his mask fell out of the bag and rolled several feet in front of him.

The whole market went quiet and a crowd of people were staring at the mask. Ray quickly picked it up and put it back in the bag. It was a very tense moment and getting the mask out of sight was critical.

With the war situation heightened the city was as tense as piano wire and chemical poisoning was most feared amongst the families that lived there. The guys did not want to stir up the locals' fears by displaying their masks.

Tony was just in the market looking for a blanket to send home. He was not looking for a situation, but as fate would have it, one happened anyway.

As Tony was weaving his way through the throngs of women, beggars and merchants, he and Ray got separated, and an old bent over Bedouin man bumped into him and stood his ground. Before Tony could say he was sorry, the hooded man, not really looking at him, said in a low voice, "$800 USD."

Tony wasn't sure what he was hearing but the old man continued. "$900 USD for your mask soldier-man, and $1,000 USD for any others you might have. We know who you are, he said. You are the soldier from the Embassy that was trying to mask the women and children. We were watching you soldier-man, but you didn't notice."

Tony backed away, fear rising in his throat, but the man moved forward.

"$500 USD for any mask old or not working, we can fix them."

Tony slowly shook his head and stepped back, looking for his partner.

"Wait, wait," the old man said. "Please do not fear me. Let me show you why we so desperately need what you have. Please," he said, grabbing Tony's arm. "Follow me, it's not far; and you will be safe."

Against his better judgement Tony followed the man into the depths of the market behind all the hanging blankets and shiny copper pots, into the heart of the old community that was built up around a bombed out schoolhouse.

The old man moved to a tent structure that was attached to a crumbling wall and slowly pulled back the flap letting smoke escape from a cooking pot and letting a bit of sunlight in.

It was like Tony had been struck in the middle of his stomach with something he could not see. First it was the smell that assaulted his nose, and then his eyes were ravaged, looking on the reality that was in front of him.

It was a small dark room with a cooking pot in the middle of the tent that was boiling something vile to Tony's senses. A small woman sat to the side of the pot wearing all black with a veil that covered most of her face, but her dark eyes stared holes into Tony's soul.

He hadn't noticed at first, but she was wearing a surgical mask, a very dirty one. "Is she ill?" Tony asked the old man.

"No soldier-man; look closer. She is trying to protect herself from the war that is coming. When the missiles fall from the sky and the deadly gas covers the land, we will protect our families anyway we can."

Tony looked closer into the tent and as his eyes became accustomed to the dim light inside, he saw the horror of the reality he could have never believed unless he saw it first-hand. There were four children huddled in the back in the dark, holding each other in fear of seeing a white man in their home.

Tony took a deep breath, "oh my god," he said quietly. They were wearing gas masks, old gas masks; masks from World War I and II and in various states of repair, some even missing canisters.

In the corner of the tent there were a pile of these old masks. Tony recognized them as coming from the Soviet Union and Czechoslovakia. They even had some American masks that didn't look too bad.

"We buy these on the black market," the old man said. "They can be very expensive. We know some are very old, but there is nothing else." He hesitated, "some are not." And with that statement the old man reached behind his robe and produced a brand new Canadian C3 Gas Mask!

The old woman next to the pot moved slightly and produced three more masks just like the one the old man was carrying. One of them was still in the box!

Tony was shocked beyond belief. "How did you get these?" he managed to choke out.

The old man finally lowered his hood to reveal a leathered, tired old face with few teeth and a long grey beard. "We know that your mask is the best there is soldier-man and we are prepared to buy them at any price."

"But how--" Tony asked looking directly at the man "I just released them to the Embassy yesterday."

"Money, soldier-man; money blinds a man to their reality and enough money will see them selling their safety and the safety of their families."

Tony was stunned by this remark. People were already selling their masks on the black market, not even thinking of what was ahead of them. Tony finally realized his situation and became very nervous.

The old man saw this, "you're under my protection, solder-man, so you will not be hurt; but what you carry is more precious than water in the desert right now. Most of our people have these masks," pointing to his children. "Some now even have the new mask," as he held it up. "Some do not. That makes them dangerous as the war gets closer."

They continued on and looked at two more tents that were in the same situation. The kids had the worthless masks and the parents had paper masks.

Our children must be saved, soldier-man, at all cost.

Tony looked at the old man and answered him directly "I'm sorry, I can't help you."

"Come," the old man said, "we have to leave now. I can only guarantee your safety for so long. Don't come back soldier-man. You will not leave alive if you do."

Tony could feel countless eyes staring at him from the darkness in the compound, but they weren't looking at him. He knew they were staring at his gym bag.

The old man brought Tony back to the centre of the market and in a wink of an eye was lost from view within the mass of people going about their daily routine.

It took Tony another ten minutes to find Ray. He had found an outdoor café and was happily eating a kabob thing that Tony thought might be camel.

He was sweating hard when he got up next to Ray and his friend could see that Tony was really stressed and wide-eyed. "We have to get out of here now, Ray," Tony managed to get out between breaths.

Ray knew that Tony did not get worked up easily so the situation had to be grave. He did not ask and they were out of the market in less than a minute.

In the truck, on the way back to the camp, Tony told Ray what had happened and what he had seen. "This is serious, Tony," Ray said as he was trying to process what he was hearing. "We have to report this right away."

They drove back to the camp in silence and reported to the Commandant. Lou was also in the room and hearing this ordered the stores rooms be put under guard and the Embassy notified of the black marketing right away.

Tony spent the next hour or so explaining what he had seen to the Officers and an order went out that evening putting the markets off limits until further notice.

Chapter 59

One Day to Go! The headlines read. Bush has given the "Go Orders" to his Generals.

It was 2335 and Tony lay in his bunk in the dark and thought of Rebecca and Sadie. They had to have been listening to this madness too and he hoped she was not worrying about him, but he knew she would.

Tony drifted off to sleep thinking of home and holding his gas mask.

He woke to the sound of iron on iron, vehicle movement and men shouting orders.

To Tony it sounded like his worst nightmare. "Were they being attacked?" he thought. He shot out of bed and yelled at his roommates at the top of his lungs "get ready!" Nothing more had to be said.

They were fully dressed in their chemical suits and masks and out the door in a heartbeat.

What they were greeted by was not guns blazing, missiles incoming and jets streaking by but the sounds of construction and heavy equipment. The camp was in full gear fortifying the walls and adding more barbed wire to the front gate area.

New observation towers were being erected and forward gun in placements were being dug outside the main gate. There were men with guns everywhere and they looked like they weren't messing around.

"What was happening," Tony wondered. "What had changed since last night? Had Saddam attacked, instead of leaving like he was supposed to?"

By Tony's watch he still had 18 hours until the deadline. The guys removed their masks and suits and went over to the Mess Hall which was now the centre of information.

Tony soon learned that the American Forces camp that was located a hundred yards away was moving forward into a combat zone to wait out the deadline and the Canadian camp was remaining in place, so they had to fortify their position.

Tony and his team spent the rest of the day working in the camp, moving sandbags and laying wire near the walls. When they weren't helping with camp defences, they were setting up their own detection equipment to ensure that a chemical strike would be detected if needed. It was a long hot day and the guys ate and drank in shifts.

It was 2345 by the time Tony and his team got back to their trailer. The camp had been turned into a fortress. There were armed men everywhere. Tired, dirty and exhausted, they lay on top of the sheets, staring at the ceiling. "Do you think it will happen tonight, Tony?" Steve asked in the dark.

"I don't know, Stevie, it won't be long and we'll know."

There was an unexpected knock on the door and as Tony rose to answer it, he looked at his watch, 2355.

Tony opened the door and found Lou standing there in the shadows. "Just thought we should be together," he said, "we've come a long way." Everybody agreed and Lou came in, sat down and opened a juice box.

They all sat silently in the dark with the door open, waiting for history to begin.

Midnight rolled in quietly but for the sound of machinery moving around from the American Camp.

"What do you think is happening, Captain?" Terry Sheer finally broke the silence.

"The Americans are moving forward into the Saudi oilfields, Operation Desert Storm has begun!" Lou said quietly in the dark.

"What about us?" Steve's voice showed a little tremor.

"We sit tight, until we get further orders and try to stay calm." Lou stayed another half hour and then said good night. Before he disappeared into the darkness, he called out "keep it together guys, we'll talk in the morning."

Tony finally laid down in his bunk thinking about Rebecca. "She must be going crazy by now," he thought.

It was 0500 and for all the hype and stress that had been going on leading up to this day, it was strangely quiet. "We're in the wait mode," Tony thought.

The Qatari Police had closed the roads in and out of Doha and Bahrain and the camp was officially locked down. Only personnel that worked at the Command Centre, on the airfield a hundred yards away could leave the camp, but only to work.

Tony's secondary duty was the Command Centre. Being an AD Tech as well as an NBC Specialist, he was trained in manning a surveillance scope and watched the jets move toward Saddam, and Saddam's jets moving towards the coalition's jets.

The biggest rush he got was watching the Scud missiles of Saddam Hussein being fired from unknown areas toward Bahrain and anything else Saddam wanted to destroy.

Once the Scuds left their launchers, Tony could see their heat signature and he tracked them as they moved across the screen. Computers could then calculate their path and predict points of contact in seconds. This was when the American Patriot Missiles would be launched from hidden locations to track the Scuds until they collided in the air and exploded, or not. The Patriots were great at what they did but not all the Scuds were destroyed and some got through.

Tony got to watch this drama play out on the screens and advised the Command Cell when Scuds were being launched and at what targets. Saddam's action of sending out the Scud Missiles was an act of war!

Tony was working what seemed to be around the clock now and carrying his weapon everywhere. Tension was very high, jets never seemed to stop flying over the camp and armed patrols were constantly going out.

Tony's shift in the Command Centre was now 12 hours long, 0800 to 2000 or the reverse. The guys had nicknamed the sleep time "Bagdad Bedtimes," because you just didn't know when you might sleep again, or for how long.

Two days had gone by with little else than work and sleep. The American jets flew out at night and returned by dawn from wherever they were tasked to go.

TV had been following the nightmare constantly and had been showing pictures of the devastation that had been inflicted on Saudi Arabia and the people that live there.

Tony knew Rebecca would be watching it too.

On one of the work nights Tony found himself standing in the dark, just outside the Command Centre at about 0300 trying to get a breath of air when the sky lit up in the distance with tails of fire seemingly appearing from the horizon and moved in different angles across the sky.

The silence of the moment was destroyed as missile sirens went off all over the airfield and Command Centre and for a split second Tony froze. He had to remind himself to breathe normally as he grabbed for his mask and put it over his face. He had never been so scared in his life. There were actually Scud Missiles, incoming. "Control your breathing! Control your breathing!" he kept screaming at himself in his head.

Getting to the scope was the best thing he could do. It calmed him as he sat at the screen and watched the Scuds arc up into the night and slowly change directions individually.

The Computer screen came alive with information about the four missiles and identified their targets. Two of them were heading for Bahrain, one for Doha and the last one was heading for the Canadian Airfield, home of the Canadian Air Division!

Chapter 60

With the number of jets from different countries flying in and out, it was only a matter of time before someone noticed where all the damage was coming from and got pissed off.

"What's the fly time on the Scuds, Sergeant Simons?" the Flight Commandant asked.

Tony checked his readouts from the computer and answered quickly, "two minutes, sir, and it looks like we own one."

The Commandant made a quick call and everyone except key personnel were ordered to shelters immediately.

Tony then saw new activity on his screen; four more heat signatures appeared from nowhere and headed right for the Scuds. Time seemed to slow down. He watched as the Patriot Missiles on the screen slowly arced up into the night sky, locked on their targets and moved in to destroy them before they got to their intended locations.

Fifty-nine seconds, fifty-eight, fifty-seven, fifty-six; Tony watched the slow dance unfold on the screen. The Patriots moved in on the two Scuds that were destined for Bahrain and engaged.

Fifty-four, fifty-three, fifty-two; contact made. Tony saw the first Scud disappear from the screen. The second Patriot moved in on the second Scud, but seemed to falter and missed the target.

The Commandant ordered the second Patriot destroyed in mid-air so as not to explode on the ground. Unfortunately, the second Scud found its target. It was a mosque and was leveled to the ground.

The drama continued on the screen, forty-five, forty-four, forty-three. The third Scud, targeting Doha was destroyed just inside the harbour, creating little damage.

Thirty-nine, thirty-eight, thirty-seven; one left and it was heading for the airfield and the Command Centre. An Air Defence Location or Bird Gunner, as they were known, had radioed in that they could see the Scud fire arcing through the night, making for the airstrip.

Tony was watching his screen and could see the Patriot moving in on the Scud. The Commandant came up behind Tony to watch the drama play out. "It's going to be close, really close," he said.

Twenty, nineteen, eighteen, seventeen; the Patriot's flight was true. Contact was made at eleven seconds. The explosion was deafening and shook the ground around the airstrip like an earthquake.

For a second the airfield and the Command Centre went dark; then the emergency generators kicked in. Everything went dead silent as the smoke on the runway cleared and everyone in the Command Centre started to breathe again.

"That was too damn close, gentleman," the Commandant said. Tony didn't answer right away. He hadn't stopped shaking in his suit or sweating in his mask.

The war had really begun and for the next five days Tony was either in the Command Centre, sleeping or running for his shelter in the middle of the night to the sounds of sirens, jets screaming overhead or automatic gunfire from out in the desert.

The only word they were getting was the American Forces were pushing the Iraqis back and the next day the word would change again and they would hear that

Saddam's Generals were fighting back and making headway.

The air battles were intense and jets were being shot down on both sides. Saddam had put a bounty on any downed American pilot that survived and Tony could only guess what that meant.

"Desert Storm" was in full forward battle mode and both sides were taking casualties. Sniper fire became the norm in and around the Canadian Base and it wasn't unusual for machine guns to open fire in the middle of the night driving Tony to his shelter for hours, masked up, rifle loaded at the ready.

Scuds were being launched regularly at Bahrain and the oilfields around them and the airfield. Sometimes the night was lit up with so much tail fire from the Scuds and Patriots you'd swear it was New Year's Eve. All you could smell was burning buildings and gunpowder. The air wasn't clean anymore and smoke drifted over the desert constantly and choked lungs so bad masks had to be worn.

As Tony looked out into the desert toward Doha and the devastation he knew was happening there, he wondered if the children there had survived the shelling and the choking dust. He also wondered about the Ambassador and his spoiled young wife. He would probably never know.

Tony sat on his bunk and wondered how long he had been in-theatre, weeks, months? It felt like forever.

Word was going around that a small Iraqi force was secretly moving in on the airstrip and things were going to get worse. The sirens went off every night. They just didn't know when an attack would happen.

On one night, Tony was in the Command Centre around 0200 and he had already run to his shelter four times. The Patriots were doing a good job, but they weren't perfect. Two Scuds had exploded in and around the airstrip and one destroyed a jet that was in a small hangar causing a massive fireball.

Fire fighting efforts were going on everywhere. As a jet from the French Forces was attempting to land, it was fired upon with a Laws Rocket from a hidden location and that sent the ground forces into a frenzy. The sniper was located and killed where he hid.

It was obvious now that the enemy had infiltrated their defences and a deadly battle would soon commence. Anything that moved from the airfield to Tony's encampment, which was only a hundred yards away, was under heavy guard or an armored vehicle.

More news coming in had Saddam ordering his Generals to fight to the death and send the Americans to Hell!

Saddam was pushing harder than ever into Saudi Arabia and claiming oil wells along the way. Saddam needed the oil wells to pay for his war and he would have them at any cost.

Endless days and nights of missiles and gunfire also led to days and nights of much needed silence. It was hard to explain why this happened but Tony looked forward to the quiet, no matter how unsettling it was.

The camp was now 1200 strong with all the new troops coming in and the number of jets flying in and out was hard to fathom.

The airfield had become a major forward strike area and also a high priority target for the Iraqi Forces.

All the reinforcements and equipment couldn't stop a lone driver in a small van that one dark night from driving through and exploding himself and the truck up against the main gate.

The gate shattered and razor wire concrete and injured men were everywhere. The attack had begun.

Chapter 61

Sirens and alarms went off at the same time and hundreds of men scrambled from their bunks, weapons in hand heading to the breach and their defences.

Tony had been enjoying a few hours of uninterrupted sleep when the explosion went off and sent him sprawling to the floor. "It's happening now," he thought, and he was part of it.

He was already dressed, so it was only a matter of masking up and checking his weapon. All his guys were up and with him as they ran, low across the compound to the shelter they knew so well.

Men and equipment were everywhere and there was live fire coming from where the main gate had once been. Tony could tell from the direction of the flashes that the enemy had taken over the old American Camp and were firing on the Canadians from the safety of the walls there.

Tony dove into the shelter just in time to see the ground to the left of him disappear under a huge explosion.

He sat in the dark of the hole, holding his weapon pointing to the opening, waiting for whatever might happen. "Don't move," he told himself. "Stay still, wait, wait."

Then it happened again, the ground just outside the door exploded throwing concrete and dirt into the air, leaving Tony gasping in his mask as the concussion of the blast pushed his back against the wall.

Steve was the first to yell over the blasts that were coming in. "Mortars, they're using mortars Tony and they are peppering the compound!"

Tony barely heard his friend over the blasts. He was aware of what was happening and was sitting there; waiting for the next round that might take the shelter out and everyone that was in it.

He noted that he was unusually calm with what was happening around him and found himself thinking about why he was here and whether or not he had done a good enough job and was it enough to get him through.

More mortars exploded behind the shelter and heavy gunfire was coming from his right. For a moment he thought of Rebecca and how lucky he was to have her in his life and how she would raise Sadie alone if the night ended badly. He shook his head and got back into the present as men began yelling and cheering outside.

"What the hell was going on?" he thought. He moved to the doorway and crawled out of the shelter, thinking if he was going to die tonight, it wasn't going to be in a hole.

The mortars had stopped, light gunfire could be heard, but not like it had been only moments ago. He moved his head over a berm just in time to see two Canadian F16 Fighter Aircraft destroy what was left of the old American Base with their Tomahawk Missiles and automatic gunfire creating an inferno.

A massive cheer went up all around the camp and Tony and his guys eventually found themselves sitting on top of their shelter, masks off, looking at each other in disbelief.

Tony shook his head, "come on guys, we have to find Lou." Then off they walked into the darkness.

Two days later the camp had repaired the walls and determined men manned the new gun in placements.

Tony and Steve were once again in the Command Centre early in the morning watching the massive Scud activity on the screens and the Patriots' response. It seemed heavier than ever before and Tony could swear there were fifty or more Scuds in the air at one time. Then suddenly the Scuds stopped launching and the Patriots did what they could do.

The screens started to empty out and in time the last Patriot destroyed its target. Strangely, there were no more. It was eerily quiet.

"What's going on?" Tony asked.

The phone rang loudly in the quiet in the Command Centre and the Flight Commandant answered and listened intently. Then he hung up the phone and quietly walked to the centre of the room, looked at his watch, it was 0401. "Gentlemen," he said, "the war is over. Saddam's Generals have surrendered in the desert and their forces are retreating as we speak. We will stay on high alert until ordered to stand down, but for now, all I can say is well done."

Chapter 62

It took a day or two for the message of the surrender to get around to all the ground forces but eventually all the sniper fire stopped and the desert was quiet once again, all except for the wind.

Word came from Command that Saddam's forces were indeed in full retreat, but at a great cost. They were burning the oilfields as they left and the Saudi Arabian Desert nights were lit up like daytime with thousands of oil fires spewing toxic gas and black smoke.

Saddam Hussein was in hiding and could not yet be found, it would only be a matter of time before he would be brought to justice to answer for his war crimes.

Chapter 63

Since Tony left Rebecca's new norm was going to work, where she would hear of the progress in Qatar and finally the start of the war. It was everywhere, at work, on billboards, newspapers and of course, the news.

After work she would pick up Sadie and try to keep things as normal as possible for her until she went to bed. Then Rebecca would watch the news. When finally exhaustion took over she would go to their bed and let the tears fall, praying it would be over soon.

Rebecca heard it at work first. Saddam's Generals had surrendered! Then after some time she learned that Tony would be coming home!

Chapter 64

Life was getting better for Tony. He had talked to Rebecca that morning and told her again and again that he was ok and would be getting back to her and Sadie soon. He was just waiting for his orders.

She cried on the phone and told him she loved him, missed him very much and told him to get his ass back to her as soon as possible!

Things never move fast in the military unless it's someone else's emergency. He was close to getting there a couple of times but weather, breakdowns and other shit got in the way.

It took a total of 10 days for Tony to finally receive his orders and run onto the waiting Hercules.

As he sat in his cargo net seat clutching his kitbag and box lunch, he watched as the tail cargo door rolled up and closed, knowing that he had just experienced something that would stay burned in his memory forever.

A feeling of pride and accomplishment washed over him and for a brief second in time Tony pictured his grandfather wearing an old Air Force uniform, sitting in the cargo net seat across from him. "You did good, grandson," he could hear him say. "I'm proud of everything you have done. You have brought honour back to the family name." With that he gave Tony an approving smile and a wink. That wink, he remembered from so long ago. He then faded away.

The giant cargo plane's engines came to life and in a minute Tony was in the air. The plane banked hard right and the Captain came over the speaker "take a last look out the window guys; we are just over the camp now."

Tony didn't need to, that part of his life was done.

Twelve hours later he was descending into Lahr and in a few minutes more, he would be in Rebecca's arms once again; it had been forever.

Chapter 65

On the ground, taxiing up to the AMU, Tony's face was pressed against the glass. He could see throngs of people waiting there, but no Rebecca.

Tony walked down the loading ramp, out onto the runway to be greeted by sunshine and humidity; he was home. He walked towards the crowds of people and still wasn't seeing Rebecca and wondered if she'd been delayed.

Suddenly out from behind the crowds of people and under a barrier ran Sadie yelling "Daddy! Daddy, Daddy!"

She was wearing this pretty little yellow dress with white flowers and a big pink wide brimmed hat that was, at any moment going to fly off because she was running so hard.

Rebecca had seen Tony getting closer and hung back for a moment and let her excited daughter break through the crowd and run towards her daddy. The hat now gone, Sadie flew into Tony's arms and he felt at peace again. She hugged him forever and he picked her up and moved toward the crowd. "Where's mom?" he whispered in her ear.

"She's behind all those people over there," she pointed. As he moved closer, the crowd thinned out and there she was. Tony's world stopped as he looked upon her for the first time. She was dressed the same as Sadie, a beautiful yellow dress with small white flowers and a big pink hat. She was stunning!

She finally broke through the crowd and waving madly, ran into Tony's arms to be completely engulfed by him. After a massive hug and a kiss that went on forever, they finally stepped back to breathe and hug again.

"That was a lifetime," she finally said. "Don't do that again!"

Tony smiled at her as they moved toward the parking lot.

There were plenty of people there that wanted to stop and talk to Tony but he had had enough of the military for awhile and wanted to go home. He had been granted two weeks off and was going to fill it by being with his family and tucking his daughter into bed every night.

Being with Rebecca had always been magical but their time apart had uncovered a burning desire that was impossible to quench. The two weeks together were the happiest they had ever had.

When he walked back into the office two weeks later, Tony was welcomed by the guys, as they clapped and slapped his back and he got a few hugs from the civilian secretaries.

Tony's section supervisor, Randy Moore, welcomed him back and talked to him quietly in his office for what seemed like hours before telling him that he had a meeting with the Flight Commandant that afternoon.

Tony didn't think too much about it. He knew that his boss would want to hear about his experience firsthand and would want to congratulate him personally. He had no problem with that. It was just good being back.

Tony's desk was being used as a holding area with a mess of files and paper on it, but he didn't mind in the least, he was home.

He spent the morning taking phone calls of congratulations from people he had worked with and even guys he knew back in Canada were calling to say hello and "congrats."

He phoned Rebecca at her work and told her he was having quite the morning and was the "toast" of the section. She laughed at him and told him not to let his head get too big or his hat wouldn't fit. He told her he loved her and would pick her up after work, grab Sadie and have dinner at a Gasthaus instead of cooking.

Rebecca loved cooking for Tony, but she let it go, besides, German food was delicious.

Fourteen hundred rolled around and Tony reported to the Commandant's office as requested.

As he entered the room, he was immediately aware that he was not alone. The Commandant was there, of course, but so were Randy Moore and to his surprise, a dear friend, Lou Tanner.

Tony presented himself to his superiors. "Sergeant Simons reporting as ordered, sir."

The Commandant rose from his desk and came around to shake Tony's hand. "Well done, Sergeant Simons, you made this section proud and we are deeply grateful."

Tony continued to stand at attention and was aware that Randy and Lou were to the left and right of him, with the Commandant standing in front of him. He reached out to hand Tony something that he had hidden in his hand. It was a Warrant Officer's emblem! "Congratulations Warrant Officer Simons for a job well done and greatly appreciated!"

Tony was thunderstruck and nearly fell over. He managed to choke out a "thank you, sir," and was aware of Randy and Lou taking off his Sergeant's shoulder epaulets and sliding on his new Warrant Officer epaulets.

"Congratulations Warrant Officer Simons," Lou said as he grabbed his hand.

"Well done!" Randy piped up. "Now I don't have to work so hard, I can share."

Tony walked out of the Commandant's office with his best friends to the cheers of the rest of the staff in the training section.

Tony was numb. "Can I leave early, Randy?" Tony asked. "I want to tell Rebecca as soon as I can."

"Don't ask me," Randy replied, "you and I are the same rank now. It's time to start wearing those big boy panties you had stuffed in your back pocket all this time." Randy smiled and walked away.

Tony drove to the babysitter's first this time so they could both be waiting for Rebecca to spring the news.

At first nothing looked out of the norm for Rebecca, other than Tony had picked Sadie up first and was waiting in the parking lot. As she got closer, she smiled to herself "don't they look cute with Sadie in Tony's arms like that," she thought.

As she slid in for a kiss, she was about to ask him where they were going for supper but noticed that Sadie was playing with something in her hand. She hoped it was at least clean.

Sadie handed it over to her and she looked down in her hand to see a Warrant Officer's emblem staring back at her.

The lights came on and excitement welled up in her chest, as she looked up at Tony's shoulders to see the bright new Warrant Officer's emblems staring back at her.

"Oh my god Tony," was all she could say before he drew her in and kissed her.

"We made it Becca," he said and kissed her again.

That night in the Simons home was the happiest they had ever been. It just kept getting better.

They opened a bottle of Dom Perignon and tried hard to explain how much they loved each other but there weren't enough words.

Chapter 66

Spring moved into early summer for the Simons family and in Tony's own words, there just wasn't a more beautiful place to be than in old Germany in the summertime; sunny days, warm breezes, the smell of fresh baked bread, coffee and of course outdoor markets; to be more specific, the marketplatz in downtown Lahr.

It was the most wonderful market Tony and Rebecca had ever seen. There were flowers everywhere, hanging out of windows, open air shops selling everything a tourist would want, bakeries that drove senses crazy and of course gasthauses everywhere selling the best beer in the world. Thousands of tired and thirsty souls came to this wondrous place every weekend to gather in the sun, drink beer and idly talk to their friends as they people-watched the day away.

The Platz, as it was known to the locals, was the place to be. This custom was not lost on Tony and Rebecca and they went to the Platz every chance they could.

It was a beautiful Saturday morning around 0830 when the Simonses finally rolled out of bed, mainly because Sadie was having none of this sleeping in business and launched herself into the middle of the sleeping pair and demanded breakfast.

Once Sadie was occupied with her cereal and a cartoon on TV, Rebecca returned to the bedroom to dress and make up the bed.

"What do you want today, Becca?" Tony asked as he stepped out of the shower and began toweling off. She stood back and watched him then reached for the towel to dry his back. She loved this body and she loved this man, but she needed to talk to him, it was important and today was to be that day.

"Let's go to the Platz, love," she said. "It's a beautiful day and the place should be packed.

Tony loved the Platz; their favourite place to sit, drink beer and have a light lunch was the Stork Tower. It was the centre of the market, located on four corners in an old barn-like building that was surrounded by a courtyard and a small stone wall you could look over and talk to people passing by.

Tony and Rebecca dropped Sadie off at her best friend's house for the afternoon and once at the Stork Tower they found a great table next to the wall, looking down the Platz to one of the huge fountains that could be found there.

Tony ordered a beer and Rebecca ordered a sparkling water and they were sipping their drinks, waiting for their food to come.

Tony was looking everywhere, trying to see if he could see anyone he knew. Rebecca had been quiet all this time, but Tony hadn't noticed. He was about to raise his hand to someone that he recognized when Rebecca reached over and stopped his movement. He looked over at her with questioning eyes but stopped short when he saw that she had a serious look on her face.

Panic was his first reaction, but softened as he saw her smile that little smile she had when she had something she was hiding but wanted to tell him.

"Rebecca, what's up?" Tony questioned. She squeezed his arm tighter and said that she was never prouder of him and their life together was a dream, especially in Germany.

"I couldn't see it getting any better, Tony, but I was mistaken, it has. I'm pregnant Tony, five weeks I believe. We are going to have another child."

Tony just about fell off his chair when the news finally registered, "oh my god, that's great news Becca," he managed to say. "Are you ok? Can I do anything? When did you find out? When are you due?" Emotion welled up inside him and he stood up, took her in his arms and kissed her.

All he kept saying was how much he loved her.

They sat there and talked for most of the afternoon about how their lives were going to change with two little whirlwinds running around, but it was going to be awesome, and Tony could hardly wait.

They talked about the time they had left in Germany, which was short and knew that the new addition to their family would be born back in Canada, but where?

Tony wasn't sure where he wanted to be posted, back to another Base, in charge of a section, or to the school in Borden as an instructor? None seemed too appealing to him after Germany and the Persian Gulf.

This was a decision he and Rebecca would have to make shortly, but not right now. They were having a baby!

The couple sat there for what seemed to be an eternity. The world around Tony seemed to get smaller. He only had eyes for the lady across from him. Everything else blurred out.

As they talked, Tony didn't see the two shadows coming up behind him and wouldn't have acknowledged them at all had the biggest one not put his hand on Tony's shoulder.

Tony rose angrily ready for a confrontation. He turned and looked up, tensing himself but was caught off guard by the big smile that looked back at him.

Tony's recall was immediate, Sam Higgins, and to his left another familiar face, Dan Blocker; the RCMP officers that were in Doha with him at the Embassy.

"May we sit down? Sam asked."

Tony was still reeling from this chance encounter and of all places, Germany. "Please sit down, guys," he replied. "You haven't met my lovely wife, Rebecca. We're celebrating. We're going to have another child."

"That's wonderful news, Specialist," Sam said and Tony answered him with "Tony, just call me Tony."

"Congratulations Rebecca! Really great news, you must be very excited."

"We are Sam, it's a great day," Tony beamed.

Tony took a second or two to look closer at the two big men sitting across from him and questions came to his mind.

From the Persian Gulf to Lahr Germany, after three months to meet, by chance in a beer garden surrounded by thousands of people; what are the odds of that? Tony's answer was easy, not good at all.

"What are you and Dan doing here Sam?" Tony probed. "And don't try and give me that coincidence business."

Sam's face broke out into a wide grin and Dan lowered his face and chuckled to himself. "Well you're kind of right there Tony," Sam went on. "This isn't a chance encounter. We were looking for you."

Rebecca reached over and held Tony's arm. Sam saw the reaction from Rebecca and calmed her fears. Sam leaned over toward him and smiled. "We want to offer you a job, Specialist."

You could have knocked Tony over with a feather. Once he came back to his senses, he answered, "I have a job, guys. Haven't you noticed? I'm in the military."

"That didn't go unnoticed Tony. Neither did how you handled yourself over there and the conditions we had to endure. You were a professional and a caring person all at the same time. That was noticed too. When we got back to Ottawa and were being debriefed, your name came up many times."

"What you do is special and unique, something you don't see every day and hope you never do but it happens and the public is better off not knowing about it, which is why we are here. The government is starting up a new taskforce that will operate quietly in the shadows so as not to panic people. We are here to ask you to become part of that taskforce, working alongside me and Dan here and a few more guys that are interested in meeting you."

Tony was floored and didn't know what to say and Rebecca, hearing this was sinking her nails into his arm.

They sat in silence for awhile, looking at one another. Then Sam rose up from his chair, reached over and shook Tony's hand. "The offer is out there Specialist, don't wait too long to make a decision."

As the two men started to leave Sam turned and congratulated Rebecca again, then he said "Specialist!" and Tony stood up. Sam continued "Congrats on the promotion!"

Glossary

AMU	Air Movements Unit
BDF	Base Defence Force
CANEX	Canadian Exchange
CD	Canadian Depot
CFB	Canadian Forces Base
CFS	Canadian Forces Station
CMP	Canadian Modular Protection
DMCC	Data Maintenance Control Centre
MIR	Medical Inspection Room
MP	Military Police
NATO	North Atlantic Treaty Organization
NBCD	Nuclear, Biological, Chemical Defence
NCO	Non-Commissioned Officer
PMQ	Private Married Quarter
WOC	Wartime Operation Centre

We are excited about our new writing project that will be out in spring 2020.

Catch the progress on our blog at Prairiewriters.net

About the Authors!

Warrant Officer, Retired, Larry Edward Crandell, CD Medal; NATO Peacekeeping Medal; Gulf War Medal with Bar; Kuwait Liberation Medal; Order of St John's Medal.

Larry completed 25 years in the Canadian Military, working first on Radar Sites, then for NORAD as an Air Defence Technician. He then worked as a Nuclear Biological Chemical Defence Technician working for

NATO in Germany. He is a Veteran of the Gulf War and was there when the night skies lit up as the missiles rained down on Bagdad. Larry spent many nights during the alerts alone in his shelter, out in the desert, writing journals about his experiences and wondering what he was doing there. He completed his military career as the Standards Warrant Officer at the Nuclear School in Borden Ontario.

Once retired from the military, he spent a few years working in the Alberta Tar Sands and teaching in Fort McMurray; he retired in Saskatoon, Saskatchewan and spends his time writing with his lovely wife of 39 years, Shirley.

Born on the prairies of Saskatchewan, Shirley's career of 35 years was in administration where she took to writing Newsletters and Standing Operating Procedures; and she has always enjoyed writing. She met Larry in 1980 and travelled the world with him and daughter Kathryn. Now retired, she has the time to spend on her personal passions, writing and jewelry making. She has previously published a non-fiction book called "Through the Fog."